THE BOOKWORM AND THE CAT'S MEOW

JEANINE LAUREN

Littleford House Books

ISBN: 978-1-0689038-0–9

Cover Design by 100 Covers

For animal rescue workers everywhere. Thank you for doing such important work.

CHAPTER 1

*R*aven Windsong Johnson walked into the Abbotsford cat shelter with an empty cat carrier. "Hi, Joanne."

A woman of about forty-five stood bent over the reception desk, staring at some papers, her hands pushed into her hair. Raven recognized that look. She often felt like tearing her hair out, too.

Joanne looked up from the reception desk, smiling through her exhaustion. "Thank you for coming so soon. I'm sorry you had to come over from the island, but I didn't know who else to ask."

"It was a good excuse to visit my sister. She doesn't live far from here, and we both had the weekend off. I also retrieved a pair of three-week-old kittens from up the valley. Part of that kitty mill raid the humane society pulled on Friday."

"The Russian blues? I heard the conditions were horrendous."

"Truth is, I would have come over here just to help with those."

"Still, I appreciate you taking Sebastien. He would thank you too if he understood that he's almost out of time here. The ornery old so-and-so." She motioned to Raven to come behind the counter and follow her through the door to the cattery, where felines of all colors and sizes slept, groomed themselves, paced, or simply watched them pass.

At the end of the corridor, a large orange cat stood, his tail switching back and forth as they approached.

"Well, hello, Sebastien," said Joanne, holding out some treats to the cat.

He backed away from her as she opened the door to his cage, arched his back, and spat from a safe distance in the corner.

"What happened to him?" asked Raven, her heart going out to the terrified animal.

"They found him all alone after his owner died. We were told he was downstairs when his owner had a heart attack in his upstairs bedroom. We aren't sure how long Sebastien went without food and water, but he was hungry and severely dehydrated."

"Poor guy."

"When the emergency responders came to take away the body, he ran under the house. It took the neighbors a good two hours to coax him out with sardines. I have some cans for you to take with you. According to the neighbor, they're his favorite, and they seem to calm him down. He needs to be rehabilitated, to learn to trust again, before he can be adopted. But as you can see"— she waved her hand toward the rest of the cattery— "we are well over quota, so we haven't enough time to spend with him."

Raven placed the carrier inside the door while Sebastien huddled far in the corner. "Got any of those sardines?"

"I'll get you some."

"We'll have to get you onto a more regular diet, Sebastien," Raven murmured, "but in the meantime, we'll give you your comfort food. Sounds like you've had enough change for a while."

The cat's ears perked up at his name, and Raven felt his yellow eyes watching her every move. Joanne came back a few minutes later with a small dish of sardines and Raven placed it into the carrier.

"What do you think?" she asked the cat. "Want to try your luck with me?"

Sebastien hissed at her but then licked his chops and stared at the sardines.

"I haven't fed him yet today. Thought we may need to convince him to go with you."

"Well, boy. What do you think?" Raven said softly to the cat. She backed away so he would be comfortable approaching the food. "Two hours to lure him out?" she asked.

"Yes, but the conditions were different. He was in a familiar home and probably felt safe there. He hates it here. He might see the sardines in a box as the lesser of two evils."

The doorbell rang, indicating that someone entered the reception area.

"You look after that." Raven nodded toward the door. "I'll stay here and get better acquainted with my new friend here."

Joanne headed toward the front desk. "How can I help you?" she asked just before the door swung shut behind her.

Raven slid to the floor and spoke calmly to the cat. "Well, Sebastien, it seems you've been through a lot. You must feel abandoned. I would be angry too."

The cat swished his tail back and forth, but more slowly than before. His eyes darted between Raven and the food and back again. "I understand," she said conversationally. "I was abandoned once myself a few years ago."

Mreoww.

"Yes, really," said Raven. "So, I won't abandon you. You can rely on me."

She kept talking, watching the cat from the corner of her eye as he crept closer to the food, stalking it as he would a mouse. Keeping her tone neutral, she told him about her daughter Wren, who now lived in Calgary with her friend and worked in a vet clinic. She told him about her sister Drew and the play they'd watched

Saturday night. She told him about the pair of tiny gray kittens waiting for them in the back seat of the car.

"We should go soon," she said. "That pair needs to be fed every few hours."

The cat crept ever closer to the food in the carrier. Only a few more minutes of speaking to him should do it, as long as no one came to interrupt them.

"Hey." A young man came in at the end of the corridor.

"Hi, Skyler," said Raven in a calm voice. "He's almost into the carrier. Would you mind getting me an old towel? I have another pair in the back, and I need to make sure he can't get to them."

"Sure," he said, stepping backward the way he came in. "I'll tell Mom you need a bit more time."

"Thanks," she said, spinning back to the cat, who took the opportunity of her distraction to dart into the cage and snatch up a sardine.

"Oh, no you don't," she said, pulling open the door to his cage and shutting the door of the carrier behind him. *Mrowl.* He whirled around and spat at her.

"I'm sorry," she said. "You have to come with me. You

wouldn't like the alternative." Then, more loudly, she called out, "Okay."

The door creaked open, and Skylar peeked in. "You got him?"

"Yes."

"Great. He can be pretty nasty. If it weren't for sardines, we'd never be able to clean his cage. Here's the towel."

She took it and picked up the carrier. Sebastien continued to yowl his dissatisfaction, poking his paws out the side of the cage to swipe at her.

"I have a trolley," said Skyler. "We can put the carrier on that and wheel him to the car."

"Great idea," said Raven, glad for an option other than carrying the angry cat. He hadn't managed to scratch her yet, but it was only a matter of time if she carried him so close.

Skyler came back a few minutes later with a wheeled cart, and they placed the cage onto it. Sebastien spat again, and she murmured to him as they pushed the cart to the parking lot, and she opened the hatchback to her Subaru.

"You're going to be fine. Cats like it at my place."

Mroww, he said again as she transferred the carrier to the car. In another cage already in the back, two tiny kittens curled up together, watching the drama as their new seat mate joined them.

"Don't worry," she said to the pair. "He's just scared. You will all be okay." She covered the part of the cage where the twins lay snuggled together, so they were out of Sebastien's line of sight. Then she stabilized the new cage and placed a pillow between the two to ensure they wouldn't shift in transit. "There," she said to Sebastien. "You're going to be just fine."

Yeowl, he said, his protest softer than before. She closed the door and noticed through the glass that he was now focused on the remaining sardines. "Ah, you were right about his weakness for sardines, then. Good to know."

"Yep. He's not so bad once he has his fish, but he hates it when we bring in any potential families to match him with. He's going to take a while," said Skylar.

"Fortunately, my last special case recently found a home, so I have time to give to my new friends." At least she hoped she did. A lot would depend upon if she could fund a larger shelter so she could take in more paying borders and keep paying her staff. But she had a potential solution for that, provided things came together as planned.

Footsteps crunched on the gravel, and she turned toward them.

"Thanks again," said Joanne, handing a box to Skylar and motioning for him to put it in the car. "These are the sardines I told you about. We really appreciate it. If there is anything we can do to help you sometime, just call us."

"I will," said Raven. "Now I'd best get going or I'll miss the two o'clock ferry."

"Do you have a reservation?"

"Wasn't sure how long it would take to pick up Sebastien, so I didn't bother," said Raven, slipping into the driver's seat and looking up at Joanne. It's just an ordinary April Tuesday."

"True," said Joanne. "Safe travels."

"Thanks," said Raven. "I'll send you an update in a few days." She snapped her seat belt on, and Joanne wished her a final farewell before closing her door.

"Well, you three, time to take you home." She started down the long drive to the main road. When she paused to turn into traffic on the main street, she listened for a few moments, and was grateful not to hear a reply. With luck, the trio was settled for the journey.

CHAPTER 2

*L*ance Reed stood on the corner of Pender and Burrard in downtown Vancouver and scanned the street for his daughter, Zoey. She should have been here by now, and he hoped she wouldn't stand him up like she had eighteen months ago when he was here last.

At least today the weather was decent. Last time he'd stood under the nearby awning in the driving October rain for half an hour before Zoey texted to say she had a work emergency and couldn't get away.

He'd returned to the airport drenched and discouraged —and wracked with guilt that the message he wanted to share in person would now be delivered over the phone. He and her mother were getting a divorce, and that meant they were selling the home where Zoey and her sister Chelsea had spent the past ten years and dividing all the contents and proceeds.

Zoey hadn't come home since that strained call, the excuse being work and then courses. Chelsea, his younger daughter, hadn't taken the divorce well either. On the rare occasions she visited him, she was often silent and sullen. Though Marlene and he had explained their decision, Chelsea blamed him for the divorce. Any time she did speak to him, she would tell him he should have listened more often and tried harder.

According to Chelsea, he was at fault because he tried to solve his customers' problems instead of paying attention to what was happening at home. If he hadn't been so focused on work, he would have noticed and understood when Marlene, his wife of twenty-five years, began to drift away.

He looked up and down the street again and ran his hand over his short, cropped head. Where was Zoey? Did she blame him, too?

Did she also not understand how much he and Marlene had tried? They'd spent four months in mediation, talking everything through, trying to save what they had worked so hard to build. But their marriage had run its course.

Marlene wanted her shot at a career selling real estate and buying houses to upgrade and flip. He wanted a peaceful life in one place, with shelves that held books rather than the latest trendy knickknacks that went with the color schemes she chose. He wanted to go fishing in his camper every few weeks.

She wanted new, up-to-date furnishings, bright colors, and networking parties. He wanted his grandfather's old leather chair, wood-paneled walls, and silence. After running a plumbing business for thirty-five years, cleaning up the mess other people seemed to make of their homes, and being on call half his life, he wanted time to think, to read, and to be.

So, after several weeks in conversation, they decided to part ways and move on. Marlene and Chelsea stayed in Toronto. Chelsea would visit him in the summer, and he would go out there near the winter holiday break to stay with his brother and visit with her.

They would review the situation when she headed off to university the following year and figure out when they could see each other. If she wanted to see him.

He didn't think Chelsea missed him as much as he missed her. At seventeen, she was about to enter her last year of high school. She worked after school and on weekends at a local pharmacy, volunteered at the pediatrics hospital, and had an active social life. She would be gone to university in eighteen months.

Maybe he should have stayed, found an apartment, kept running the business. But in the six months he'd spent renovating the family home, updating the kitchen and bathrooms and putting in new floors so their profit would be larger, he had never been so lonely. Even if he could have bought Marlene out of the house, nothing would ever be the same.

Their old life was done, and he didn't want to think about it anymore.

He searched the street again for any sign of Zoey, then checked his cell phone for a text message, though he hoped she wouldn't bail on him again. It would be several weeks before he could return to Vancouver, and he wanted to see her. Though they spoke on the phone several times a month, the calls were brief, and she often seemed distant. It would be better once he saw her, spent time with her, had a chance to finally talk about things.

At least he hoped it would be better.

No texts from Zoey. Where was she? He hoped she wasn't held up at work again. Though if she were, she would cancel their lunch again. He and Marlene had modeled that habit. When there was work, they worked. And though they scheduled their time so at least one would be home when the children needed them, they hadn't made their own relationship a priority.

He checked his watch again. She was fifteen minutes late now, so he scrolled through his email to see if she had sent something to him that way. Reading emails might help him stop replaying the last few months in his mind.

Marlene had heard about mediation from a friend of hers who used it. Though he'd been reticent at first, those ten sessions helped them really "see" each other for the first time in years. It allowed them to part on good terms. But he wondered how many marriages broke down because of nothing other than poor scheduling. Especially schedules that put the couple last, after financial stability and their children's needs.

"Dad!" He whipped around and there she was, strolling toward him. His little girl, now twenty-one years old, dressed in smart casual rather than the sweatpants she used to wear when she helped him on the worksite or when they watched a Maple Leafs game together. This Zoey was the vision of a professional woman, and he beamed with pride as he walked to meet her.

She stood up on tiptoes and hugged him tight. He squeezed her back, trying to convey in the gesture how much he missed her. How important she was. "How much time do you have for lunch?"

"They gave me an hour because you're here. And there's a great place to grab fish tacos nearby."

"Lead on," he said at the mention of their favorite meal. Chelsea and Marlene hated fish tacos, so it had become a Zoey and Lance tradition, and it pleased him that she remembered. As they approached the restaurant, he could see it was popular.

"Looks pretty busy," he said. "Is there somewhere else?"

"I got a reservation for eleven forty-five," she said. "Axel, a guy I work with, suggested I do that."

"Smart guy."

"Yes, he is," said Zoey, blushing, and Lance was surprised by a flash of jealousy. Like any parent, he knew his daughters wouldn't need him one day, but it didn't mean he had to like it. And when Axel's name came up twice more over lunch—once when she talked about their joint project and once when she described the various restaurants they'd been to together—it became clear to Lance that this man was becoming important to her.

"Sounds like you're enjoying this last work placement," he said.

"I love it. When I went into marketing, I never thought about tourism, but it's been fun. I've met people from other countries, and I'm applying for a job that would give me the opportunity to travel internationally and market our province to the world."

He smiled, but a sense of loss crept into his chest. It figured that, as soon as he gave up his whole life in Ontario and drove across Canada to start his new life on Vancouver Island, his daughter was thinking of leaving. She was one of the main reasons he'd come this far.

"I may not get it. But I hope I do."

"How much travel is involved?"

"About six weeks a year," she said. "But otherwise, I

would be here, or visiting Chelsea wherever she ends up. She wants to go to McGill."

"Yes, she has a good chance. Her grades are high enough, and she's doing the volunteer work she'll need to apply for medical school," he said. "Though secretly I wish she would apply to go here to UBC, instead of Montreal."

"You never know," said Zoey. "She's got almost a year before she applies, and it is best that she has more than one option. If she came out here, I'd like it too. I miss her."

"Do you speak with her much?"

"No. Usually it's Mom who tells me how she is doing, which basically means I listen to Mom brag about her. You know, Chelsea aced a test, Chelsea got a new job at the hospital, Chelsea this, Chelsea that." Zoey rolled her eyes good-naturedly. "Can you imagine what she's telling people at that golf club she joined last year?"

Lance smiled. "Your mother is proud of you both. As am I."

"Oh, I know," said Zoey. "But there's a certain cachet about having a child who wants to be a doctor. Business and marketing aren't as prestigious, are they?"

"Chelsea has always loved medicine, and I'm sure she'll be a brilliant doctor if that's what she ends up doing. But by the time she finishes her education and sets up a practice, you will be in the position to help her and to give her the advice she may need," said Lance. "She'll need business skills."

"Never thought of it that way," said Zoey. "Thanks, Dad. You always know what to say."

"I've learned over the years that you need to be happy doing what you're doing. Though life is short, it can seem long when you're doing something you hate."

"Is that how you felt about plumbing? Did you hate it?"

"No. I didn't hate it. I just outgrew it. When I started working for my uncle, I was only eighteen. Then when he got sick four years later, I took it over so I could help support his family and my mother. And then your mom and I got married, and you and Chelsea came along. It was a solid career, and it paid well. Did what it needed for the family."

At the mention of family, her gaze flew to his face, and he shifted his focus to the taco he was eating.

"How are you doing, Dad? You sure you want to give up the big-city life to live on an island?"

"Aww, are you concerned about your old dad?" he teased, pushing down the sadness that threatened to overwhelm him whenever he remembered the good times. Times like that would never happen again, and he still thought he'd somehow failed his girls.

"Yeah, kind of," she said. "I mean, it's a big move, Dad. Giving up the business and all your friends to come to the other end of the country and buy a bookstore?"

"I'm looking forward to it," he said. "Besides, Aunt Betty may still back out of the deal. She wants me there today to go over the papers one more time before she signs the sales contract."

"I never thought she would retire," said Zoey. "Though I guess it's been about five years since I last saw her. How old is she now? Sixty?"

He chuckled. "She passed that age about fifteen years ago. She was my father's junior by about four years, I think, and Dad would have been seventy-nine this year."

"Really? She aways seems so young and energetic. I can't picture her ever giving up the store."

He laughed. "Neither could I and, as I say, she may still

back out. She's got some last details she wants me to agree to first."

"What kind of details?"

"No idea, but if I know my aunt, they will involve community outreach of some sort. I just wish I knew what I was getting myself into." He took another bite of the delicious taco. "My cousin Nancy once had to wear a pink tutu for one of Betty's launches of a series of ballerina books. Poor kid had to spend the day posing, hand-selling the books, and pasting a perma-smile on her face. She was so mad when a boy she liked witnessed her in her costume." The more he thought of Nancy's horrible day, the more he wondered what Betty had up her sleeve this time.

"Oh no. That would be so humiliating," said Zoey laughing.

"But Betty just pointed out how many books they'd sold and told her it would help build character." He took the last bite of his taco. "These are some of the best tacos I've ever had."

"They are pretty famous in these parts," she said. "Listen, Dad, I was thinking about your bookstore. One of my first co-op placements was in retail. If you ever need some help brainstorming marketing angles to go with these community projects, let me know. I'm sure one reason she is so involved in the community is to market the books."

"I may call you sooner than later on that."

"But if it's pink tutus, leave me out of it," said Zoey.

He laughed. Zoey took her last bite of taco and added, "I'm sure whatever she wants to discuss is minor. It'll work out. If all else fails, you could start a plumbing business again."

"Oh, please," he groaned. "After thirty years of cleaning up other people's crap, I am done with that. No, I look forward to selling and reading books. And I imagine I'll find something to enjoy even in whatever Betty has up her sleeve."

"You could go fishing if it all gets too much."

"Yes, come and join me one weekend. It's been a long time since we took a fishing trip together," he said.

"That sounds fun. And I'm super excited to see the store."

"I just hope it doesn't involve pink leotards and a tutu," he mumbled.

Zoey snorted. "It'll be a whole new world, Dad."

He joined her laughter. The other patrons were staring at them, some with annoyance, others with a bit of envy, and he realized he hadn't laughed like this in months.

After he paid for their meal and walked her to the front entrance of the skyscraper where she was working, she hugged him again, and he watched her go until she was out of sight.

Pleased that lunch had worked out so well, he turned toward where he had parked his truck so he could get to the ferry terminal. Traffic would pick up soon, and he had only an hour to check in to claim his reservation.

Zoey was the only reason he had to visit this city, and he was looking forward to getting to Sunshine Bay, where he had spent several weeks every summer growing up. He had never felt so much at home anywhere else, and he owed it all to Aunt Betty. She had made his tumultuous childhood calm when he needed her most, letting him work with her in the store while his father was away for work.

At the parking lot, he noticed a dent on the driver's side door that had not been there three hours earlier, and his positive mood faded again. Great. Now, on top of moving costs, dividing assets with Marlene, and purchasing his aunt's business, he would have another bill. He wrenched open the truck door and climbed in.

He couldn't get to the island fast enough.

An hour and twenty minutes later, he was driving up the ferry ramp and into the bowels of the ship. The stress that had knotted up his shoulders smoothed out. In less than two hours, he would be at his destination.

He rooted around in his backpack before remembering that he'd left his book in the back of the camper. He opened the door and climbed up the steps but nearly tripped over a flash of orange that flew past him and into the camper.

"What the…?"

"Sebastien, come back!" He turned to see a woman dressed in old jeans and an oversized shirt, her black hair scraped back in a severe bun, running toward him with a wild look in her eyes.

CHAPTER 3

*R*aven ran in the direction Sebastien had bolted, wishing she'd remembered to put water into his cage before she left the shelter. She should have known he would try to get away.

A big man with short-cropped hair stood in her path, and she drew to a quick stop before she rammed into him.

"Did you see a cat run past?" She peered up at him. He was big, but not overweight as a lot of men in their fifties were. Just a large person. With muscles. And a tattoo of an anchor and a wheel on his forearm. She stepped back, feeling overpowered by his presence.

"It jumped into my camper." The man nodded to the doorway.

"Oh, no," she said, running a gloved hand over her face.

"That's a nasty scratch," he said, pointing at her arm.

She turned her arm over and looked at the long thin line of blood forming there. She used her other hand to dig around in her pocket until she pulled out a balled-up tissue.

"You can't use that," he said, frowning at her.

"I'll be fine. It happens." She glared at him, wishing he would just let her get on with things. She needed to return the cat to the car before the ferry crew came.

"Come here. I've got a first aid kit in the back." He climbed into the camper and came back a moment later. "Sit down for a minute." He motioned to the foot of the steps, and she shook her head.

"I need to put Sebastien back into his carrier. They don't allow passengers to stay in the lower car decks during the sailings."

He just looked at her calmly, opened the kit, and pulled out some gauze and antiseptic.

"I'd feel better if you would let me help you. He's under the table. I saw his tail twitching. Not a happy traveler, I guess."

She let him gently take her arm, surprised at herself. She hated it when men took over. Duane, her ex-husband, did that, and it always put her back up.

"Really, I'm fine," she said. "I have to get the cat."

"Almost done." He continued to clean her wound. Why was she allowing this? Because he was so forceful? Concerned? Attractive?

She needed to get the cat and leave. Now.

"There," he said. "That should do it. All cleaned up."

She looked at her arm and she saw it was indeed clean. The blood had stopped. "Thank you," she said. "I'll grab his cat carrier and I'll be right back."

He said nothing, just stood back and looked at her in a steady way that made her unaccountably nervous. "I'll be back in a minute."

"I'll wait," he said, his deep, sonorous voice sending a shiver through her.

She hurried back to the car, determined to be done with this man as soon as possible. She grabbed the cage, checked in on the sleeping kittens, and grabbed another can of sardines from the box.

When she returned, the man opened the camper door, and she stepped up into the small space. There was a bed over the cab of the truck, a small kitchenette, and a table with benches on both sides, décor and style from the 1990s. How did he even fit in here? The man was enormous.

She set the cage on the floor near the table and peered underneath. Sebastien crouched in a corner, watching her, his tail clicking back and forth like a pendulum, counting off the beats until he would leap—or attack with his claws—again. Her arm still stung from their last encounter. Or maybe it was from the antiseptic. Probably both.

"Is he still under the table?" a deep voice asked from close behind her. She shivered. She would need to keep her distance. Something about him felt danger-ous. He reminded her too much of her ex, though she couldn't quite put her finger on what they had in common.

"He's still there. I just need to coax him out."

"What do you usually do?" Did he sound impatient?

"No idea." She turned to find him leaning in, watching her, and she immediately regretted her move. The eyes. That's what he had in common with Duane: deep brown eyes with flecks of gold she could explore for hours. She swallowed hard and held up a can of sardines. "He's a rescue I picked up a couple of hours ago, and the only thing I have tried so far that worked is sardines."

"What happened to his owner?"

"Died." She opened the can, set it into the cage, and shoved the whole thing closer to Sebastien. "Come on, boy. We don't have time for this today."

Grrrr.

"Excuse me folks," said an unfamiliar voice. "Sorry, but you can't stay down here during the sailing."

"We're trying to get the cat out," she said, trying to control her voice. She wanted to whine in frustration like a child rather than the fifty-four-year-old woman she was.

"I'm sorry, ma'am. He'll have to stay put until we finish the crossing."

She reached toward Sebastien to see if she could grab him by the collar, but the cat flattened his ears, spat, and swiped at her with his claws. She yanked back her hand.

"He's not ready to come out. I'm sorry about this," she said to the bigger man.

"Can't be helped," he said. "We'll have to try again later."

She climbed out of the camper, and the ferry worker, a young man who couldn't have been much over nineteen or twenty, looked relieved. Perhaps he thought they would cause a stink.

The older man turned to lock the door behind her. "I'm going to grab some coffee," he said. "Would you like to join me while we wait?"

"Let me grab my wallet." She walked to her car and opened the passenger door to pick up her purse and e-reader, taking the opportunity to peer at Sebastien's reluctant host. He was about six-three, and broad. He reminded her of a wrestler, and she winced inwardly at the idea of spending any time watching that sport. Not at all her thing. The sooner she could retrieve her cat from that man's camper, the better.

When they got to the passenger deck, they joined the line for the cafeteria, and she was grateful that it was moving quickly. When they finished with their coffee, she could find a place to read for the rest of the crossing.

They stood side by side. He stared straight ahead while she looked out at the ocean.

So, he differed from Duane in one way. Duane talked all the time and could convince anyone to see his side of things. It was why he'd been so good at securing venture capital for their business—and how he'd convinced her to marry him.

In contrast, her current companion was the strong, silent type. As much as she hated a big talker, she hated the strong, silent type more. You never knew what went on inside their heads.

She finally broke the silence. "I'm sorry about the cat."

"Do you have a plan to get him out?" he asked.

"I'll go down as soon as they announce that we are allowed to. We'll have a few minutes before the ferry docks." She stepped forward in the line that was beginning to move a little more quickly.

"I don't know how you can spend time with cats." He looked down at her, brows drawn.

"You don't like cats?" Who didn't like cats?

"No. They bring nothing but trouble," bending down to pick up a food tray from the stack of trays at the entrance to the cafeteria.

She picked up a tray as well and decided to change the subject. "Where are you heading?"

"I've got a meeting in Sunshine Bay this afternoon, and then I'm heading up to Campbell River to do some fishing for a few days."

"I used to go fishing with my dad," she said. Until she joined her sister at university on the mainland. Neither of them went home much after that.

"My buddy has a boat, so we're going salmon fishing this time," he said. "How about you? You live on the island?"

"Just outside of Sunshine Bay," she said. "I have a farm, and I also rehabilitate and board cats."

"What do you grow on your farm?"

"Hay. It's a relatively easy crop to grow and only needs to be harvested once. And I have a kitchen garden where I grow what I need for the year. It saves on groceries. Also about thirty chickens, which give enough eggs for me and for my staff."

"What do the chickens think of the cats?"

"We don't keep them in the same vicinity, so it would be a rare cat that would see them."

"Always wondered what it would be like to run a farm," he said. "But I grew up in the city, so if it weren't for my summers here on Vancouver Island, I wouldn't have any exposure to rural life, much less farms."

"What do you do in the city?" she asked as she picked up a salad from the refrigerator and placed it on her tray.

"Plumber," he said.

So not a wrestler. She stepped into the line for the drinks, poured a coffee, and then paid the bill. "I'll grab a table."

"Sounds good," he said, pouring a coffee for himself.

Raven carried her tray toward an empty table and sat down facing the cash register so he could find her.

None of the other passengers looked as tired as she felt, and she still had three more weeks of frequent kitten feeding to go. She closed her eyes a moment, wishing she could fall into a deep sleep under a warm blanket.

The next few weeks would be busy.

CHAPTER 4

*L*ance paid for his coffee, then walked over to where the cat woman sat. He needed to introduce himself and find out her name. "Cat woman" wasn't appropriate, and besides, that name was already taken.

He set his tray down across from her. "I'm Lance," he said, sitting. "What's your name?"

"Raven."

He grinned.

"I know. A woman with a bird name looking after cats. Believe me, I've heard it all."

He chuckled. "I'm sure. How did you get into farming and cats?"

"Kind of fell into it, really. After my divorce fifteen years ago, I bought a farm. I wanted a life as different from what I had as I could get. I grew up on one of the smaller Gulf Islands, and I missed being on the land."

"What were you doing before you bought the farm?"

"My ex, Duane, and I started an educational software business. He was the creative force, and I was responsible for managing the staff and accounting. The software was a hit, and we were able to sell the business for a good profit."

He didn't say anything, though he wondered what had happened with her marriage. She seemed angry, even after fifteen years, and it surprised him.

"When he wanted to put together another start-up, I realized the only thing we had together was building businesses. He appreciated me for my ability to manage the details, but our personal relationship just wasn't working. My priority was our daughter Wren. His priority was Duane. So we split our sales from the software and residuals as part of our divorce settlement. Each of us came away with enough to start over. He used his to invest in another tech company, a risky start-up without a good managing partner. I advised him not to, by the way, but he did it anyway."

He said nothing. Why did some women do that? Feel the need to run down their exes? He hoped Marlene wasn't doing that, though he had to admit she might be. Chelsea blamed him for the divorce, and though he didn't really blame anyone, maybe Marlene still had hard feelings.

He hoped not. Marlene wasn't normally one to discuss such things with their daughters or even with friends. Though he had noticed several of their friends had stopped interacting with him. That was another thing that bothered him. Why was it that some people took sides even when the couple was trying to keep everything amicable?

He turned his attention back to the conversation, and though Raven was attractive and seemed nice enough, he was glad that they would be parting ways soon. She still seemed bitter about her divorce and likely wasn't making room in her life for others. Besides, she sure talked a lot.

All he wanted to do was go fishing with Del after signing papers with his aunt. He planned to come back on Friday night, move into his new home over the weekend, and get started at the store on Tuesday.

In a month he hoped to be completely settled into his new life, and by the end of June he hoped to have everything running so smoothly that he would have time to spend with Chelsea when she arrived in July.

"I came out to Sunshine Bay because Rosalyn, my best friend from college, was living there," Raven said. "Wren and Rosalyn's daughter are only a few months apart in age. We both needed to start over, so we decided to help each other out. Rosalyn is a vet, and she and I started a kennel and vet practice on the farm. Then over time, we began to take in rescue cats, a few at a time. She lived with me on the farm with our daughters until about a year and a half ago, when she remarried. The kids had already moved out to Calgary to pursue careers working with animals."

"That's a lot of change," he said.

"Yes. Now it's me, the cats and chickens, and a whole extra house next door that I rent to Mal and Daisy, two of my staff. When they leave, I'll probably renovate it."

"Renovations take a lot of time and energy, in my experience."

"I know. And right now, I can't imagine renovating another building. I've been working on the construction of a larger kennel near my house so I can take in dogs and have more space for the rescue cats. It's going slowly. Hard to get the tradespeople. You must be in demand, with your skills."

"True. Plumbers are never lacking for work these days," he said. She didn't need to know anything else about him and, unless she specifically asked, he wouldn't say. Though she was attractive, independent, and had the capacity to care—at least about her daughter and animals—she wasn't his type.

He wondered, then, who *would* be his type. Did he even have a type? Because Marlene, his wife of three decades, apparently wasn't his type either.

They finished their coffee and she said, "I thought I would find a place to read my book. It's been a long weekend, and I need some downtime before we get there. You are welcome to join me if you like."

Though the idea of sitting near this attractive woman and watching her read was momentarily appealing, he had an itch to get away for a bit, to get some exercise. "I think I'll take a walk around the ship, but as soon as we can go to the car deck, I'll meet you downstairs so you can get Sebastien."

"Thank you," she said, looking relieved. She didn't want to spend more time with him, either. Good. At least he knew where he stood. Even if she had been his type, he was smart enough to know that when a woman shut you down, you needed to walk away. Life was too short to waste on lost causes.

They parted, and he pushed open the door to the outer deck. It was cool outside, but the sun was out. He walked around the deck three times, then paused to lean on the railing and look out at the islands as they passed. The wind ruffled his hair as he watched for whale spouts and seals.

He was glad to return to the island. It felt right, and after so many months of having to make hard decisions.

~

*R*aven was the first to return to the car deck, so she quickly checked in on the kittens. They were so tiny, their ears still plastered against their wee heads as they bobbed around looking for food. She looked around for Lance and decided to feed them while she waited.

When she had returned the first kitten to the cage and started feeding the second, Lance emerged from the stairwell. She worked to maintain her focus on the cat rather than on the large, muscular man strolling toward her. He seemed to shift the energy around him, and her eyes were drawn repeatedly in his direction. Really, he was impossible to ignore.

"What you got there?" he asked.

"I picked these two up this morning. They needed some extra help, and I said I could assist."

"He's tiny. That must take some patience." He was frowning and looking at her oddly.

"I have the time and resources to help, and I love looking after the little ones. Whenever someone has a few, I get a call to see if I can help. It would be best, though, if people would just get their cats spayed or neutered. There are so many cats left without homes. Or, in the case of these two, being bred by people who keep them in deplorable conditions."

"How old?"

"Vet figures three weeks."

"They're lucky to have you," he said. "Not many people would spend so much time looking after abandoned cats."

"I find it satisfying. And when they're ready, we'll find them a new home."

"Do you ever keep them?"

"Not often. I have one right now who, like Sebastien, had a hard time adapting to others. Jackie is a tabby, and I have built up a rapport, but she's pretty picky about whom she will have as her housekeeper. It's something Wren, my daughter, and I laugh about. Dogs have owners, and cats have housekeepers—or slaves, depending on the day."

"Cats and dogs have their differences for sure. My last dog was a German shepherd. Very loyal, and my girls loved him."

She wanted to ask him about his girls, but decided it wasn't necessary. They would never see each other again after they left the ferry. She placed the now well-fed kitten back in the cage beside its sibling, and the pair curled up together again and drifted off to sleep. "Let's get my other charge, shall we?"

He led the way back to the camper and unlocked and opened the door. Then he stood back, waving his arms in front of him. "What is that stench?"

Raven peered in and drew back, immediately feeling sick. "I am so sorry, but he must have sprayed somewhere."

She peered in again to find Sebastien curled up in the carrier, the empty dishes of water and sardines sitting beside him. "You little devil," she muttered, then quickly leaned in, latched the door of the carrier, and pulled him out. "Listen, if you stop by my farm, I can wash it out for you. My staff is great with cleaning up after cats, and we have some effective soap and cleaners for the purpose. It's only about ten minutes from the ferry, and then you can be on your way."

He considered her offer, all the while looking at her with those dark brown eyes. What was the guy thinking? Was he angry? Did he see the humor in this? Did he have any opinion at all?

"I'll take you up on that since I don't have cleaners that can do this justice and I have to sleep here tonight," he finally said. "Give me your address, and I'll follow you."

She pulled out a business card and handed it to him. "The address is on the back. And again, I am so sorry about this."

"It's fixable," he said, his face like stone. "They're unloading. We should get back in our vehicles." Then he turned and strode toward the driver's side of his truck.

She watched him walk away, then quickly put Sebastien's carrier in the back of her car and climbed in her car just as his taillights came on and he started driving.

She edged the car forward until she was out of the ferry, down the ramp, and onto the road. A few minutes later she caught up with his truck, pulled into the right lane, and passed him so she could get home and ask Mel, the employee who was on shift today, to get a bucket of water and soap together. She felt bad about inconveniencing the guy.

If she were in his shoes, she would not have been this reasonable.

CHAPTER 5

*R*aven's Subaru sailed past him, out of view, and Lance had half a mind to keep driving—until he remembered the smell. He couldn't stay in the camper until it was cleaned.

Since her car was no longer in view, he pulled over to the side of the road to enter her address into his phone. When he found his destination, he followed the directions off the highway and down a country road until he saw a large sign that marked the entrance to Happy Tails Kennel and Veterinary Services.

He turned onto a long driveway lined with forest on both sides, and drove for more than a hundred yards before he came to three buildings: two houses—one with a wing connected to it that housed the cats—and a large outbuilding in the lock-up stage. That had to be the expansion she'd mentioned. Beyond the buildings lay a red barn and freshly plowed fields, and beyond them, the sea. He whistled under his breath. That software business of hers must have been a roaring success.

He pulled up beside her car and found a pair of young women standing on the gravel with rags and a bucket of soapy water.

"Raven says we need to clean up after the new cat," said the younger one, a slight blonde with baby blue highlights, and cat tattoos on her forearm.

"I'm Mal," said the other, a woman in her late twenties, with a dark pixie cut, "And this is Daisy. It may take about forty minutes. Raven said to send you in for a cup of coffee while you wait. She's just getting the new cats settled in. She'll be there in a minute." She motioned for him to go inside the rancher while her partner walked to the back of the camper. He walked around and unlocked it to let them in.

"Wow, the little stinker," said Daisy. "He must have been mad."

Lance grunted in agreement.

"Go on in," Mal repeated. "We'll take care of this for you. It will be good as new when we're done. Promise."

He left them to it and walked toward the house. But before he knocked, he took another minute to breathe in the sea air, gaze out over the property, and really appreciate the beauty of the place.

He glanced back at the camper. They had already opened the windows, cranked up the roof so they could easily stand inside, and were hard at their task.

Another cup of coffee. He didn't need more caffeine today, but he had to do something while he waited so he knocked at the cabin door and heard her say, "Come in."

He turned the handle and held his breath, expecting to step into a cluttered space that smelled of animals, like many he'd seen during his life as a plumber. Instead, he stepped into a bright, open concept home done up in white and neutral colors. Large floor-to-ceiling windows graced the wall facing the sea, and French doors opened onto a back patio. A nook was built in the wall off the kitchen, and he imagined Raven there, enjoying coffee in the morning and contemplating what she needed to do that day.

At least that was what he would do if it were his home and his day to contemplate.

"Coffee or tea?" she asked from a bright white kitchen that Marlene, who was very particular about kitchens, would have adored. There were features similar to those he'd added to his last home because, according to Marlene, it would increase the value. Fortunately, the buyers had thought so too.

"Could I just have some water?"

"You sure? I can brew something up fast, and I'm making myself a decaf anyway."

"Okay, a decaf," he said after reconsidering. "Thanks."

She turned on the coffee maker. "Do you take half and half? I'm out of skimmed milk."

"That's fine. But no sugar."

She opened a door and reached into a built-in fridge. Nice detail, he thought. The sleekness of the home made the relatively small space look much larger.

The coffee maker stopped its gurgling, and she poured coffee into a pair of blue-and-white mugs with cats on them and brought them to the table in the nook. Then she went back to the counter and picked up a plate of cookies. Fresh chocolate chip cookies, judging from the smell that filled the room.

"When did you have time to make these?"

"I was at a market on Saturday and picked up this homemade cookie dough my sister raves about. Thought I would test them," she said. "Want one?"

"If you want it to have any scientific significance, more than one person should test it," he said, never able to resist a chocolate chip cookie.

"Don't feel you have to," she said. "That lot outside will be happy to help test cookies."

"I don't eat a lot of sugar," he said. "Diabetes plagued my dad in his last decade, and if I can avoid that experience, I will. But these smell great, so I feel I need to make an exception."

She smiled. "My parents are the opposite. We never had sugar growing up, so neither my sister nor I can resist a cookie, though I don't eat as many as I did when we went to university. I think I gained twenty pounds my first semester before I learned the source of my problem."

She took a bite of her cookie, and he picked one up from the plate and bit into the warm, gooey middle. "It's a good thing they're only sold on the mainland," he said after a moment. "These are so good."

"Right? I love chocolate chip cookies. And the best thing is, the tub of dough will freeze for a few months, so I don't have to hurry through them."

They sat in silence, eating first one and then a second, gazing out toward the ocean. "You have a marvelous place here," he said.

"Thanks," she said. "I just had it redone last year, kind of a make-work project after Wren left and Rosalyn moved in with her husband. I was trying to take my mind off them all leaving at the same time. It was a big adjustment."

"It's hard to face kids growing up. My eldest daughter, Zoey, is living in Vancouver. Doing well. I took her out for lunch today. Chelsea, my youngest, is still living in Toronto with her mother, but she'll be heading to university next year. I could have stayed another year, I suppose, but I had a great offer for my business, so I decided it was time. She'll visit me out here."

"Out here? You mean you're moving to the island? I thought you were just camping."

"Yes, if the business I'm looking to buy works out. But meanwhile, I'm looking forward to catching up with some old friends and family I have here."

"Raven?" said Mal from the doorway. "We're finished, but…"

"But?"

"Come and see."

Puzzled, they both rose to follow Mal to the camper.

"We've scrubbed down all the surfaces, but we can't seem to find the source. Doesn't appear to be the bedding. Maybe you can figure it out."

Raven climbed into the camper and stood in the middle of the room. Lance poked his head in to see what was happening. The place looked cleaner than he'd had it in years. He thought a little dust when camping was to be expected. The scent of the place was now soap with a hint of chlorine and a fair amount of cat piss.

The sea breeze blew through the window, and he knew immediately what the source was, though she still seemed to be puzzled, looking around at the floor area.

"The curtains," he said. "I think he's sprayed the curtains."

"We'll have to wash those." Raven leaned over to the curtains and tried to take them down.

"I can do that. Don't worry. It'll be fine."

"At least let me wash them for you." She removed one and began working on the next.

"I should get going. I'll find a place to wash them when I'm on the road."

He climbed up, stepped around her, and removed the other offensive-smelling curtain. As he turned to face her, she reached out and grabbed it. "I insist. I'll mail them to you. Really."

"I should just replace them. They're practically thread-bare," he said, tugging them back toward him. Rather than let go of her end, Raven gripped it harder, and before he could just let her have her way, they heard a loud *rrrrip*, and Raven lost her footing and went flying into the seat of the camper kitchenette.

"Are you okay?" She looked close to tears.

"I ripped it."

"Just throw them out. Then I'll be on my way to the campground, and you can move on with your day. It must be nearly time to feed the kittens again." Why was he talking? He always talked too much when he was around an attractive woman. Gut reaction.

"I feel so bad about this," she said.

"You have no control over what a cat does. And it's only a curtain. I have an extra towel I can put up there for the weekend if I need it."

She pulled herself up off the seat, and he wished he had climbed out again. The camper was a tight fit for him when he was in here alone. Something about her proximity was messing with his equilibrium, and now she was standing only a few inches away, her chest heaving from the exertion of pulling the curtains and struggling to her feet.

She looked indignant, not unlike how the cat had looked when she'd tried to coax it out from under the table. He backed up and found the stairs to climb down from the camper, then moved away to leave her plenty of room to follow him.

She stepped down and handed off the scraps of fabric to Daisy, asking her to take it into the laundry and giving

Mal instructions to wipe the camper down around the counter and window before they were done.

Mal climbed in before he could stop her, and he stood there, helpless to get going until she was done. All he wanted to do was leave this strange encounter with the cat woman and get on with his trip. He couldn't wait to meet Del at the campground. He needed a campfire, a friend, and a drink. At least he would have a story to tell tonight.

But first he had to get to Sunshine Bay and meet his aunt. She would wonder what was taking him so long.

CHAPTER 6

"So you made it in one piece," said Aunt Betty from behind the counter of The Bookworm by the Bay.

"That I did," said Lance, walking around the counter and stooping to give her a hug. "I had a bit of a delay after the ferry, but I made it. Now what was so urgent that I had to come in person to sign these papers? Are you trying to charge me extra or something?" he joked.

"Not exactly," she said, looking as though she were hiding something. Maybe there really was a pink tutu in his future.

"You haven't changed your mind, have you?"

"Nope. I moved into Spring Valley condos last week, and Nancy was down for a few days to help me out with the move. She's been on me for years to sell the store. I can tell she's relieved you're taking over."

"I'm sure she is," he said, thinking about his cousin who hated surprises and always had trouble with her mother's schemes and ideas. He leaned on the counter to get closer to Betty's eye level.

"So what are the caveats you want added to the deal?"

"All in good time. First, come along. I have some people for you to meet."

He followed her as she rolled her wheelchair out from behind the counter and down one of the main aisles until they came to where a young man of about thirty-five was stocking shelves.

"Lance, this is Ahmed."

The young man turned toward them and smiled. Only then did Lance realize Ahmed was much older, maybe sixty-five or so.

"Welcome to Sunshine Bay," said Ahmed.

"I'm glad to be here," he said. "I spent a lot of summers here when I was a teenager."

"Usually curled up on a bench upstairs, reading books," laughed his aunt. "Where he knew I wouldn't come up after him."

"I looked after the shelves and dusted," he said, letting out an indignant grunt.

"Or at least you imagined it to be so." She turned to Ahmed. "I think you two will have a lot in common, particularly your taste in literature."

"Your aunt and I have a deal," said Ahmed. "I am not to read any books, particularly fantasy books, when no one else is on shift, and she is not to worry about the upstairs loft. I keep it stocked and tidy—well, Pinky and I do. Pinky spends the most time up there. It's where we have story hour every week."

"Ahmed is underselling his skills," said Betty. "He came to work here after he retired, and he modernized my whole ordering and tracking system. He even impressed Nancy."

This got a smile from Lance.

"And you haven't been here long, have you?" said Betty.

"Three years next month," said Ahmed. "And I have loved working here. Your Aunt runs a tight ship but always has room for new ideas and suggestions. Her newest idea is excellent. I'm sure you agree."

"We haven't got that far, Ahmed," said Betty, giving him a meaningful look that Lance recognized.

Ahmed raised his eyebrows but said nothing further.

"Come," said Betty. "I'll take you to meet Pinky."

"Good to meet you, Ahmed," said Lance. "I'm glad you're on board."

They shook hands, and Ahmed added, "No matter what comes up, I'm here to help."

"Well, if you love books as much as I do, we'll get along fine," said Lance, already feeling a kinship with this man.

"Books are my second great love," said Ahmed. "My wife Priti is, of course, my first."

"You will probably meet Priti one day," said Betty. "She stops in sometimes when she's on a work break. She's an accountant and works for the town."

"She has been given a promotion," said Ahmed proudly. "So you may not meet her for a while. But when she comes in, I'll introduce you."

"I look forward to meeting her," said Lance, and he noticed how Ahmed beamed just thinking about his wife. He used to feel that way, a long time ago, about Marlene, and felt a grain of envy buried deep in a profound sadness that he quickly pushed aside. Regret wasn't worth wallowing in. There was nothing he could change about his past.

"Now come along," said Betty." We have a lot to cover before you leave."

He followed her to the elevator at the back of the store. "How often does this need to be maintained?" he asked.

"Once every six months. I had it replaced five years ago with a newer model. The old one was nearly thirty-five years old. They said it was a miracle it lasted even half as long as it did."

"I remember getting stuck in this thing once."

"Yes, but that would have been the old one. It was why I rarely went upstairs for a few years, and I'm thankful I could trust Pinky with the children's department."

"Who is Pinky? I don't remember her." In fact, all the old staff he remembered seemed to be gone.

The door opened onto the next floor, which was decorated with strings of sparkling lights that ran from the corner to a large chair that was intricately carved like a throne. Around the throne there were three couches and several overstuffed armchairs filled with children and their parents, mostly women. They were all watching the woman he supposed was Pinky.

Pinky was a dainty woman in her mid-forties with long salt-and-pepper hair stacked up in a hairstyle that would have suited Marie Antoinette. She wore a long pink gown that could have come from a 1700s reenactment society. Pinky held a book about dragons in one hand and a heart-tipped wand in the other. She was using a different voice for every character, and every time she turned a page she would turn the book to show the pictures to the children.

Betty motioned for Lance to bend down to her level. "She's very good," she whispered. "Has a story hour twice a week, and we get some regulars as well as new listeners every time. It's a great hit during tourist season, too."

Lance nodded and watched Pinky read some more of the book. If he hadn't seen the fifteen children with his own eyes, he wouldn't have known they were there, so rapt with attention they were.

"Quite impressive," he murmured to Betty.

"I'll introduce you later," said Betty. "First, let me show you around the apartment. Then we can go to my office so we can finish our business."

They went back to the first floor, and just before she pressed the button to open the automatic back door, he noticed a tuxedo cat sitting on the top shelf in the antiquities section.

"Who's that?" He pointed at the cat, and the feline narrowed its eyes at him as though warning him to beware.

"Rhett Butler. He's a great mouser, and in these older buildings, you can never be too careful. He's another reason the kids come in. He'll often sit up on a top shelf at story time and watch them. Though I think that has more to do with the treats Pinky gives him than any wish to spend time with children."

"And are you taking Rhett with you to your new home?"

"No, he is one of those obligations," she said. "But what bookstore doesn't need a cat? Besides, Ahmed and Pinky have taken a shine to Rhett. They look after his care and feeding. No need to worry about him."

"I suppose it's just one cat," he mumbled.

She ignored that comment and rolled ahead, using a pass to open the automatic door.

"This is new," he said, commenting on the pass. There hadn't been one last time he was here.

"I found quite a few young people sneaking back here a few years ago, so I had to take precautions," she said. "Nancy made sure I got extra security installed."

"It probably gave her some peace of mind."

"I suppose, but it still feels constrictive," said Betty. "Whatever happened to the days when you could leave your house unlocked without a worry?"

"I don't think I remember that ever being the case," said Lance. "Are you sure that isn't a story people make up when they think of the good old days? Like how you had to walk ten miles to school in snow, uphill both ways?"

She sent him a sideways glance. "I don't think it was ten miles, Lance. I distinctly remember it being twelve."

He laughed, appreciating her quick humor, and followed her down the hall.

"And what's in there?" He pointed to a door he didn't remember from his last visit.

"We'll get to that. First, let's go to the apartment."

They got to the end of the hall, and she handed him the keys. When he stepped inside the apartment, he held the door open for her to come through.

"I had it painted after I moved my things out," she said. "Though I imagine you will want to make some improvements. A lot of the counters are low enough for me to use, but there are others that are higher because your uncle used to help."

Lance looked at the kitchenette and then walked down the hall to the bedroom and bathroom. It was much as he remembered but stripped of all the warmth of Betty's heavily laden bookshelves and cozy throws. The quilt that had once hung from the upper floor was gone. Though he knew it wouldn't be the same, it felt naked. Empty. A shell, just like his old home had become.

"That wall looks different without the quilt," he said.

"I didn't think you'd want that old thing," she said. "But I left some upstairs with the beds you wanted to keep. Nancy and a few friends cleaned out the rest."

He walked upstairs and into the room he used to stay in as a child. There was still the old double bed, huge for a small boy but now rather small, and two bedside tables with lamps. The other two rooms upstairs—a bedroom that had once been his uncle's study and a storage room for his uncle's tools—were empty but for shelves at the far end.

The bathroom, with a full tub and sink, dated from the nineteen seventies. Purple basin and toilet. He smiled, imagining what Marlene would say. She would be quietly horrified and then remark out loud that there was a lot of potential here.

But he wouldn't think of her. Marlene was his past, and this purple bathroom and the bookstore downstairs were his future. What happened with his future was up to him.

He walked downstairs to rejoin Betty, who was peering up at him with anxious eyes. "Is it what you thought you'd be getting?"

"It will need a bit of work, but someone recently told me that's a good way to distract yourself when you're working through a change." He thought of Raven in her newly updated space and, though he wouldn't have the view she had, there was—dare he think it?—potential. "I can work with this," he said, and noticed his aunt relaxing. "After living in my camper for the past two weeks, this feels like a palace."

"Well, it does come with a throne," she said, referring to Pinky's grand chair, and he laughed.

"Let's get this business done so I can go fishing," he said, locking the door behind him and following his aunt back to the office.

She rolled her chair to the other side of the desk and opened a drawer. "Sit down," she said, pointing to the seat on the other side of the desk.

"I got you a new chair," she said. "For the desk. Your uncle's old chair was falling apart. I hope it works for you. If not, we can trade it for another one. I just wanted something for you on your first day."

She pointed toward it, and he took a seat. "It's great. Really comfortable."

"Adjustable," she said. "But I guessed at your height and such." She seemed very preoccupied with the chair, so he assured her again that it was fine.

"You sure you're okay with giving up the store? You don't have any misgivings?" he asked.

She was bent over the file, shuffling papers in her search for something, and she looked up, startled. "Oh, no. I'm ready to give it up. It's time to try something new."

"Okay…" he said. "You seem distracted."

"No, it's nothing. I just want to make sure I haven't forgotten anything. There has been a lot to think about in the last few weeks with the move and all."

"It's been forty years since you and Uncle Stan opened this store. I can imagine it might be hard to leave it behind."

"Do you regret leaving the plumbing business behind?" she asked.

"No. Not really."

"Then I should be fine. I'm involved in a lot of things in the community and already have people asking me to help with all manner of events and tasks."

"Well, if it isn't giving up the store, what is bothering you? You've seemed distracted ever since I arrived."

"I want to ensure I haven't forgotten any details." She pulled two documents from the file folder and gave him one. "The first five pages are the agreement for the book business you already saw," she said.

"The one my lawyer looked over." He would take her comment at face value for now but couldn't help but wonder if she was telling him everything.

"Yes, nothing has changed since your lawyer went over those pages, but the marketing and community commitments are new. If you turn to page six, you'll find the addendum." She folded back the first five pages from her copy. "It's marked with a tab."

Lance turned to page six and scanned the preamble. "So you want me to honor your commitments to the community for twelve months?"

"I'm hoping you will want to commit longer, but to help the community transition, and to give you a good taste of what I've been doing behind the scenes to create relationships in the community, I think a twelve-month period would be reasonable."

Lance took a deep breath. "So all of these are commitments you made in the past, and you want me to continue to honor them for one year. Starting Tuesday?"

"Yes, until the end of April next year," said Betty. "And I need you to put your all into this, Lance. I've been building relationships for over forty-eight years. It's why my little indie bookstore thrives when so many have failed against the online giants."

"You don't need to tell me how important relationships are to business, Betty. I had to compete against some large, well-established companies over the years."

She smiled. "Yes, I suppose you did. I hadn't considered that." She looked like she was relaxing a bit. He would see what he could do to put her mind at ease, because he needed her. Betty had always been his lifeline, and without her to turn to, he wasn't sure where he would be right now. Just like when he was a child, she had given him a focus and a safe harbor, and he would be forever grateful for that.

"Let's see what you've got. Why don't you walk me though what all these items mean?"

She gazed steadily from across the desk as though trying to read his level of sincerity, then said, "Let's go through the first page. This is a list of businesses that I have worked with over the years. We collaborate where we can, and we brainstorm ideas once a month with the downtown business association."

"All these businesses are in the association?"

"The ones on the first page of the addendum, yes. I've listed the contact information on the second page."

He flipped to the next page and saw, indeed, that the downtown merchants' association included the stores on either side of this one—one that sold hardware and another that sold chocolate.

"Page three lists the projects we have agreed to," she said. "And you will see a few lines under each project that show the specifics we have agreed to engage in here."

He looked at the list. "The next event is the May long weekend?"

"We often hold a sidewalk sale. There are tents in the storage room to protect the books if it rains. And this year Pinky will work with Banjo Bill."

"Banjo Bill?"

"He's a multitalented individual," said Betty. "If there is a festival or celebration, you will find Bill there. He makes balloon animals, dresses as a clown, walks on stilts in parades, plays the banjo of course, and he is also an excellent storyteller."

"Sounds like an interesting character."

"Yes, he is," she chuckled. "I've known him for years. Anyway, I've contracted him to come and work with Pinky to entertain the kids for three hours on the Saturday. Then she will do a story hour, which brings in children and, of course, their parents and grandparents. We usually sell quite a few books. Pinky also uses the opportunity to sign children up for our regular story hour, which we tailor to themes, particularly when there are new releases that are likely to be popular."

"That sounds like a fun day, and I like the follow-through to the regular events," he said. If all her commitments were like that, he wasn't sure what she was concerned about.

"Yes, now let's go to the next one. That is for the July long weekend, the beginning of our Sunshine and Sea festival and the Dragon Boat festival after that."

"So, a nautical theme?"

"Yes, and of course Canada Day, so anything about the country can be showcased, like Canadian authors, books about the area, history, that sort of thing." They went through the whole list of upcoming festivals and commitments, and discussed how he could suggest changes or augment ideas if he came up with something else to try.

When they were done, he said, "This is all reasonable. And it sounds like some are annual occurrences already. I can commit to this list."

"Good," she said, though she didn't look completely happy.

"What's wrong?"

"Well, let's move on to page four," she said. "This list may be a bit tricky, but I've been working on these for a long time."

Ah. So this was it. He turned the page.

"The first item is about the bookmarks that are on sale in the cabinet near the cash register."

"I'll have to take a closer look," he said. "I noticed

some merchandise, but I didn't specifically notice the bookmarks."

"They are based on prints by a local artist, who sells the bookmarks for fifteen dollars each," she said.

"Isn't that pricey for a bookmark?"

"One hundred percent of the net proceeds go toward the purchase a new MRI machine for the hospital. I sell the bookmarks, put the money toward their cause, and the hospital sends customers my way. They also get me to order some books they use for education purposes."

"That sounds like a win-win."

"Yes. It is."

"What else?"

"There are a few artists who sell on consignment here. I charge them twenty-five percent to put their goods in here. Everything from earrings that look like books to a line of literary-inspired teas. Most of the paintings on the wall are by local artists. There's a new seller who makes puzzles that have cats and books on them. They're popular."

"How often do they come in with their goods?"

"At least once a month to replenish, or to take away whatever isn't selling. If they're selling a lot, then I call them, and they bring in more stock."

"Do you sell books by local authors as well?"

"Yes, I carry one or two copies from several indie authors on a shelf near the middle of the store, near the books about British Columbia and Canada."

"Who normally manages this part? Ahmed?"

"I've been doing most of it," she said. "But I have a part-time employee named Annemarie who works three mornings a week. She has taken over the tracking of those books as well as the consignment and charity areas."

"And how is that working?"

"It's been relatively painless. She has a background working in a consignment store, so she is used to keeping track of the various aspects of the business."

"This all sounds reasonable," he said, looking at his watch. Del would be waiting for him at Whisking Love, the local coffee shop, where they had agreed to meet. "I think I can agree to this. Where do I sign?"

"Hold up," she said. "I want you to look at page five first."

"I don't have a page five."

She pulled two pieces of paper from the folder and placed one in front of him.

"This is a new initiative. We haven't officially started, but the planning and preparation is underway, and we wanted it in place before the May long weekend. It started out a bit tricky, but we've ironed out all the details to my satisfaction. I've had them put a lot of mitigations in place. And it's already been very successful on the mainland. I spoke to the owner of a store over there who has been doing it successfully with five organizations for more than four years."

Why was she selling this so hard? he wondered. Then he bent over the paper in front of him and read the few lines on the page.

"You want me to do what?" He backed away from the desk. "No way."

"Lance, be reasonable," she said. "It's experimental, and it is really successful in other places. You only need to commit to six months."

"You know how I feel about cats. One is more than enough." He got up and backed out of the room.

Ahmed was standing just outside the office when he opened the door.

"She told you."

"I don't see how this can possibly work."

"She has been very concerned about how you would react to this idea," said Ahmed, his voice low. "She had me do the research. I am confident that it will work. And just think of the spin-off sales."

"But—"

"Your aunt won't tell you this, but it is sometimes an uphill battle to get people in here, particularly anyone between ten and fifty."

Lance looked at the man, who was speaking in earnest, and he listened. "Are you telling me the store is in trouble?"

"No. Not in trouble. But we constantly need to pivot and bring in different product lines and angles. This isn't like a food store, where a lot of my experience comes from. People always need food."

"They always need stories, too," countered Lance.

"Yes. But they can get them in so many other ways now. Online—which is why we sell e-books now off our website—and through serials, e-zines, audiobooks, video. Not to mention social media. You are not competing only with other print sources. There are dozens of reading apps that specialize by genre. We need to continually update, reach out, find ways to bring people into the store."

"I had thought of that, of course, but…"

"Running a community bookstore is not a nine-to-five job. We need to continually stay relevant," said Ahmed. "The business has to be part of the fabric of the community." He wove his fingers to demonstrate what he meant. "Only then will you have success."

"You think this will work?"

"I do," said Ahmed. "Especially if we can think of some interesting marketing angles and bring in spin-off merchandise." He let that settle in for a beat. "If I may ask, do you consider this a deal breaker?"

Lance ran his hand over his head. He had invested a lot already in coming here to take over the building that housed the store and the apartment attached. He had given up his old business, his old life. His belongings were on a truck headed this way, and it arrived on Saturday.

He had come too far to go back now.

"Okay. We can try it for six months." He turned to go back into the office and nearly tripped. "What the…"

Looking down, he saw Rhett Butler rubbing against his legs, and the darned cat was purring.

"I really hate cats," he said to the cat, who only purred louder. His aunt grinned from ear to ear.

"Well, they seem to like you." She laughed and handed him a pen.

He growled at the cat and sidestepped away, but the animal continued to follow him. "Let's get this done." Del was waiting and, right now, all he wanted to do was get to the campground and digest all this new information.

Betty watched him sign. "Ahmed, can you call Pinky? We can get you two to witness this."

Ahmed ran to get his coworker, who swirled into the room, still dressed in her reading costume. "Where do I sign?" she asked. "I have a few customers outside."

Betty pointed to the places, and she jotted her name and smiled at Lance. "Welcome to Bookworm by the Bay. I think you'll love it here." Then, without waiting for a response, she swirled back out of the room, and Ahmed added his name and signature as well.

"I think this will be a good move," he said to Lance. "I look forward to working with you."

"I do too," said Lance, moving a very determined Rhett Butler from his lap. "I'll see you on Tuesday."

"I'll be here for the rest of the month while you get settled," said Betty. "I'm so pleased you are taking over the business, Lance. I know it's in excellent hands."

He bent to give her another hug. "Just as long as you don't have too many more surprises up your sleeve," he said.

Four hours later, he and Del were sitting around a campfire, and he was telling his friend about the trip over and about his aunt's list of business requirements. "She's gone and made a deal with a cat shelter in town to display photos of cats that need to be adopted. Maybe even have them roam around the store."

"So, is this Raven woman your new business partner, then?"

"Oh, I don't think so. Betty would have made the deal with a larger shelter. One in town."

But for the rest of the weekend, he wished he'd asked Betty for more details. Because he had a sinking feeling that Del might be right.

CHAPTER 7

*R*aven woke up on Tuesday morning, fed the kittens, and placed them back into their pen.

"Good morning," said Beth, her third staff person who only worked part-time. "How was your trip to Vancouver? Mal says you brought home a pair of Russian blues."

"Come look," said Raven, holding open the door to the nursery and sick room area.

"Oh, they are tiny," cooed Beth. "I bet people would love to watch them grow. Did you get the webcam set up yet?"

"Not yet. I need to find someone with technical skills to help set it up—and to update my website. I'm going to meet my new partner today. I hope we can start showcasing some of our adoptees soon."

She also needed help adding a financial interface and landing page so the adoption forms could be available online. But that would need to wait until she found time to put her attention to the task. Today her priority was to meet the new owner of the Bookworm and hope they were as supportive of the venture as Betty was.

"And who is this?" asked Beth, walking over to Sebastien's pen. The cat arched his back and hissed at her. "Well, aren't you the crabby one?"

"His owner died. And it sounds like it traumatized him. Moving from a home to a shelter, and now here, isn't helping him adjust. This afternoon when I get back from town, I'll introduce him to the house. Jackie is tolerant of other cats most of the time, so I hope she'll take him under her wing and help him feel at home."

"Jackie has a maternal instinct, which is surprising for an abandoned cat," said Beth. "She sure helped the last couple adapt."

"She's my secret weapon," laughed Raven then held her finger to her lips. "Don't tell anyone, or it will ruin my reputation as a cat whisperer."

Beth shook her head and smiled.

"Listen, I'm going to be downtown for about five or six hours," said Raven. "Can you feed the twins when I'm gone? And check on old crabby Sebastien to make sure he has enough food and water. Don't open the cage, though. He's an escape artist."

"Sure. Mal and I can do it. When is their next feeding?"

"I fed them just before you arrived, so in about four hours. Noonish?"

"We can feed them before the lunch rush."

"Perfect. I should get ready."

She took extra care dressing to meet this new business partner. In her experience with business meetings, it didn't matter how talented you were—business folks often judged you by your appearance, especially if your regular garb was sweats and gumboots.

She wanted the focus to be on the project and not on concerns about whether she could successfully pull off her end of the initiative. And though Betty had assured her the new owner would agree to the partnership, she didn't want anyone to find a reason to say no. There was too much riding on this, since she didn't yet have the funds to expand the kennels and shelter. And she didn't have enough room to take on all the cats that needed help.

She drove the fifteen minutes to town on what was turning out to be a warm day, and quickly found a parking spot. When she walked into Bookworm by the Bay, she felt positive that the meeting would go well.

Betty said she was selling the store to a relative, someone she trusted, someone who valued community like she did. Raven was confident that whomever Betty had sold to would be a lot like her—always looking for win-win solutions, creative in their marketing approaches, friendly and outgoing, and, without a doubt, a cat lover. Raven had nothing to worry about.

She walked past the smaller front window, the one Betty said could display the cats, and tapped her tote bag. It carried the sketch of what she thought would work, and she looked forward to showing it to her friend Curtis later that morning. Curtis ran the local

Men's Shack, a not-for-profit organization where men with a variety of woodworking and other skills met to support each other through mental health issues while also completing community projects. Curtis said that if Raven provided the materials, he would provide the labor to put it together.

She stood outside the store a moment more, imagining how perfect it would be. Besides the front window, there was a lovely back room where Rhett Butler slept and did his business. Thanks to Curtis's club, it was already fitted with three new pens for cats to live in after store hours.

When she walked into the store, Ahmed greeted her, which she took as a good sign that the new owner had made no wholesale changes, at least to staffing. Then again, it had only been a day, so she couldn't be sure if things were likely to shift in the future.

But when she said she was there to meet with the new owner, Ahmed frowned, and her positive expectations evaporated.

Something was wrong.

"Wait here," he said, and walked to the back room.

While she waited, she took the time to scan the bookstore in search of the tuxedo cat who had inhabited the space for the past half decade. Where was he? The last few times she had been here, the cat was at the front of the store near Betty. Did that mean Betty had taken the cat with her?

She looked around the floor, down the first of the wide aisles, and then at the bookshelves, most of which didn't have room for a cat. But there was Rhett Butler, perched on the top shelf, looking down at her with interest.

"There you are," she said.

He closed his eyes as though to say, *What did you expect?* Raven relaxed again. If the cat was still here, that meant the new owner was cat friendly and would of course want to take on the project.

Ahmed came back to the front of the store and smiled at her. Another good sign. "They are ready to see you," he said. "Just go to the back office and press the buzzer." He pointed the way and then stepped away to help a customer.

She pushed the small buzzer, and the door swung open. She noticed it had a small opening at the bottom for the resident cat to walk through. She'd visited the office three times before, so she walked down the little hall and knocked on the door.

Betty called out, "Come in."

"Good morning," she said to Betty, who was sitting behind the desk as always. But the room felt decidedly smaller, colder, and less friendly.

She looked up from Betty and stumbled a little at the sight of Lance leaning against the wall behind Betty's chair, his arms crossed and his face stone, like a bouncer in a nightclub.

She quickly righted herself by leaning on the desk, and looked up again to make sure it really was him.

"Hello again," he said with that sonorous voice that sent a shiver down her spine. "My aunt tells me we are going to be in partnership for a few months."

"Your aunt?" She looked from his bouncer face to Betty's beaming smile.

"Yes," said Betty. "Lance spent many a summer in his youth in the store, and when he heard I was looking for someone who would love it as much as I do, he asked if he could be the one." She looked up at him. "I was glad to keep it in the family for however long that may be."

"Not intending to go anywhere yet," said Lance. "But then, I haven't heard all the details of this venture yet. My aunt and Ahmed both assure me there has been a lot of research done, but I'm still not clear about how it will work in practice."

"What my nephew is saying"—Betty leaned her elbows on the desk and spoke firmly enough to bring Raven's attention back to her— "is that he and cats do not have a positive relationship. Never have. He has had some, shall we say, challenges with felines. I have assured him that your cats are well behaved and will never cause him a moment's concern. We've even talked about having someone come in with them for the first few weeks to make sure everything goes smoothly."

"The cats you bring in. How will you choose them?" he asked. "As you can appreciate, I am quite concerned about them spraying the store if they are nervous or upset."

"A legitimate concern, given your experience," said Raven.

"Am I missing something?" asked Betty.

"We met last week," said Raven, determined to tell the story from her point of view. "A rescue cat I was bringing home—one who is very traumatized and would never, I assure you, be a good candidate for this venture—leaped from my car and into Lance's camper on the ferry. We were forced to leave him there for the duration of the voyage."

"The cat sprayed my camper," said Lance.

"And we did clean it up, though I know it made you late for your fishing trip. And for that, I am sorry. But believe me, Sebastien is not a cat I would bring to the store for adoption."

"How would you choose the candidates?" Lance pushed away from the wall, took a seat, and motioned for her to sit in the only remaining chair in the room. She perched on the edge like a kid in the principal's office and told herself to get it together.

"I have a female cat who lives with me, and I start off any new cats with her, allowing them to interact. I make sure they get along for a few days, and watch their habits. If they were aggressive or territorial—spraying a lot—then they would be an obvious no. But if all went well, I would bring them in and put them together with Rhett Butler. It is his territory, after all. He would have to get along with the cats too. He is mild-mannered and used to a lot of different people, but it's hard to say how he'll react to another cat. I thought we could start with one and then, if that goes well, maybe a second. But only two at a time at the most. You have a store to run, after all."

Lance was sitting back on the chair, his arms folded again, legs splayed, but he was at least hearing her out. Given his earlier experience with Sebastien, she knew she would have an uphill battle to find the right cat.

"And you want to put some in the window?"

"We thought we could put a scratching post in there, a few shelves, and a ramp or two for them to climb on. I know you have things for Rhett to climb on, but I think if we make the window theirs, it will give them all their own space."

"And what about the smell?"

"I already have a good air filtering system in here," said Betty, "because I didn't want Rhett's presence to deter customers. And the staff are very diligent cleaners."

"Well, I have to admit, the place doesn't smell like a cat lives here," he said grudgingly. He was leaning forward now, his hands resting on his knees. "What about the marketing? How do you two see this working?"

"We've given it some thought. We want to name the initiative Pages and Paws. And we could have a special adoption day once every two or three months that would bring in people looking for cats. Ideally, we could have the first one in June, as it is Adopt-a-Cat month. I'm building awareness by doing several talks about cats, how to care for them, and how to be a good adoptive cat family," said Raven. "I've already booked talks at two parent-teacher association meetings, a women's club, and the library."

"Places where parents and children congregate," said Lance, nodding his approval. "I like that idea."

"I'm also getting my website updated." She crossed her fingers as she told her white lie and hoped she could find a new site designer—fast. "We could create a page dedicated to the project and link to your site as well. My plan is to set up a webcam and add to the photos on the page. They get a lot of hits."

"A webcam?"

"When we get cute kittens in, like the blues I picked up last week, my plan is to keep a camera on them for several hours a day and film us feeding them and caring for them. Mal—you met her. She's already done some YouTube videos about cat care. We've also partnered with Rosalyn, my vet friend, who gives tips about care in return for a link to her website."

"So when do you plan to film the pair you brought over with you?" he asked. He still wasn't smiling, but at least he was engaged. Betty wasn't saying a thing, just watching them like she was a spectator at a tennis match, her eyes wide in surprise. Raven would give anything to know what was going through the woman's head.

"As soon as I get the website set up. Probably the end of the month. They will be tumbling around by then rather than just sleeping most of the time."

"And who updates our website?" Lance asked Betty.

"Oh… um," said Betty. "I do it myself. It's something else I'll have to teach you, and, truth be told, I would suggest getting a marketing expert to review it. It's been a while since I've updated the design," she said, and Lance frowned. "It still works well, and the orders come through. It just needs a refresh."

Lance looked at Betty as though calculating something in his head. "We'll have to set aside a few hours to get me up to speed on that, and I may have a line on a consultant who could help." He turned back to Raven. "What did you have in mind for the front window? Do you have the shelves and other items built?"

"My friend Curtis runs a local nonprofit that works with men who have trades skills. They are always looking for projects, and he said they would be happy to help. He's even applied to the city for a grant to help pay the guys for their time."

Lance nodded, then abruptly stood. "Come and show me what you're thinking. I just need to understand how it will fit."

Raven and Lance walked to the front window of the store. Betty, she noticed, went to the front counter to help a customer even though Ahmed was already there and Annamarie, the part-timer, was stocking shelves.

Lance opened the enclosure that separated the front window from the store. It was already set up well for the purpose. She talked him through what she was thinking and then told him about the paperwork she would leave for him to hand out to people who were interested in potential adoptions.

"When Betty and I were talking, we thought the store could hand out applications, or just a business card with a QR code so they could apply online. She was thinking you could have books featuring cats in the children's section, some books about cat care on display, and any other offshoots that we can come up with."

"Do you have any samples?" he asked.

"Not yet. Wanted to talk to you first."

"When were you thinking of doing the construction?"

"I'm meeting with Curtis for lunch. I can give you a better time frame after that," she said.

"Good. I'd like to meet him as well. Get an idea of his background and what his vision is."

"Um." she hadn't expected such an immediate, hands-on approach. "You could come with me. We're meeting at the Whisking Love bistro for lunch."

"Esther's place?"

"Oh, good, you've met her."

"Betty introduced us. Esther's quite involved in the downtown business association, though maybe not as involved as Betty would like her to be."

"Your aunt is a powerful force," said Raven in a low voice. "And Esther does a lot for the community. Sometimes it just isn't obvious. I was going to ask her about making some cat-shaped cookies if we do a kickoff for Pages and Paws."

"One step at a time. I'd like to consult someone about marketing before we start," said Lance. "But I like the idea of involving other businesses in the project. It would bring more traffic downtown while also getting your cats new homes. Betty has been telling me the number of abandoned cats has increased in the past few years. What time do you plan to meet your friend?"

"About a quarter to twelve. That way, we can get our lunch before the downtown crowd comes in."

"I'll be there," he said. "Thanks for coming in and explaining it all."

"So you'll do it?"

He sighed and glanced toward the cash register, where Betty was chatting with a customer. "I've agreed to try it for six months. Then we can review how it is working."

"And how are you planning to be involved?" she asked warily.

"I've agreed to meet this Curtis guy, and to having you use my store and my staff."

"No offense," she said, "but I've worked with people who have only given lip service to a project. Without commitment from all parties, projects like this often fail. I already know you don't like cats—and you are doing this under duress. I can look for another venue."

His arms were back across his chest now, and he was glaring at her. "I believe you signed a contract with Betty a few weeks ago," he said.

"Yes, but—"

"You should know," said Lance, his eyes narrowing, "that when I give my word, I stick to it."

"I didn't mean to—"

"I think we're done here. I'll see you at the Whisk." He turned and walked to the back of the store, taking a cloud of tension with him.

Betty looked toward the back and then rolled over to Raven.

"What happened? Why is he so angry?"

"I told him that if he didn't want to do this, he didn't have to, and he said he had given his word."

Betty winced. "Oh dear. You found one of his buttons and pushed it."

"I was just trying to give him a way out."

"Something you should know about Lance is that he doesn't give his word unless he intends to follow through. He'll give his all to this project."

"I should apologize."

Betty reached up and patted her arm. "Not right now. Give him some time to cool down. He's been under a lot of stress in the past year and, though it isn't an excuse for his behavior, it may help explain why he stomped off. Where did you leave things?"

"He's going to meet me and Curtis for lunch."

Betty smiled brightly. "Perfect. Curtis is a tradesperson; Lance is a plumber. They'll be able to talk about the project, and it will be good for him to meet more people he'll be working with. I'll come too. Just to make sure the introductions are made. We'll see you there." Then she turned her chair and rolled toward the back of the store.

Raven left feeling as though she had been dismissed. Betty would take over now, and she would just be a part of the conversation rather than leading it. Though she hated being relegated to the bench when she wanted to be leading the charge, she knew it was important for Betty to feel positive about the project and for her to support Lance.

She glanced at her watch and saw that it was eleven o'clock. If she left now, she would have a few minutes to run a couple of errands nearby.

CHAPTER 8

*H*ow dare she question his integrity like that? Lance stormed toward the office, where he paced around, trying to understand how she got the idea that he wouldn't follow through.

He listened; he asked questions. He even tried to find out more about her side of the business. The night before, he'd searched the internet to understand how many cats needed homes in the area—and he'd discovered it was a growing issue, one that was important to address.

He'd even talked to Zoey about having her come over to give him some ideas about marketing. He was sure she could find someone to help revamp the website on a budget, like a student who needed to add to their portfolio.

"Hey," said a voice from behind him.

He turned around to find Betty in the doorway. "Hey," he said.

"What do you think of the project now that you've met Raven?"

"I already met her," he said. "And I have concerns."

"Tell me more," said Betty, rolling her chair further into the room. "Maybe I can answer your questions."

He sat on the office chair and motioned for her to join him.

"She seems flighty," he said. "She comes across as knowledgeable, but she seems to lack follow-through."

"Tell me more," said Betty, and Lance scowled.

"You sound like my mediator. And I've had my fill of mediators, if you want to know the truth."

"Come on. Tell me what the problem is," said Betty.

"The first time I met her, the cat she was transporting escaped and pissed all over my camper."

"Unfortunate, but she cleaned it up, didn't she?"

"Except for the curtains," he mumbled. "Then today she comes in, talks to me about her plans, says she has ideas about written materials but doesn't have any samples with her. I want to know what I'll be giving out to the customers who ask. But when I asked her about it, she turned it around on me. Told me I could quit if I wanted to."

"And you don't want to quit?"

"I gave you my word," he said. "And you know how important that is to me."

"I do," she said. "I realize you never want to let people down. But you have the right to change your mind, Lance. I don't want you to do this if you don't want to.'

"What makes you think I don't want to?" he asked. "What did I say that makes you and Raven think I don't want to go through with this project?"

"Your demeanor." She pointed to the wall behind the desk. "You stood there like you were ready to pounce on the woman when she walked into the room."

"I did not."

"You were intimidating."

"Me?"

"Lance, don't be obtuse. You know darned well that you made that woman uncomfortable. She handled herself very well, considering."

"What do you mean, I was intimidating?"

"You stood there, arms crossed, no smile, and barked questions at her. I was going to offer you a spotlight to shine on her face like in one of those spy novels."

"Don't be ridiculous," he said. "I just asked questions. I have to know what I'm getting into, make sure she's thought everything through."

"Lance, you must know how you use your energy. You are a large man, and you take up a lot of space."

"No one ever complained before."

"No one?"

"No, I don't think so." Though he remembered Marlene telling him she felt intimidated when they first met, and he remembered others reacting to his size when he was younger. That was what he had enjoyed about working with other tradespeople. A lot of them were even bigger, so he fit right in.

"Well, I'm telling you. When you are unsure of yourself, or new to a situation like this one, you clam up. You don't smile. You cross your arms. Your questions are brief and clipped. It comes across as anger or contempt."

"Are you sure?"

"Positive."

"She questioned my integrity," he said. "Suggested I wouldn't do my best to make this initiative work."

"Listen to yourself. You are asking the same questions about her."

He rubbed his hand over his face and considered her words. Betty was wise and observant, and of all the people he had known growing up, she was the person he most trusted. Was she right about how he came across to strangers? Was he behaving differently because he felt like a fish out of water?

"Thanks. You've given me something to think about." He'd been saying that a lot, it seemed. Ever since the meetings with the mediator, he'd found things to think about, and he still wasn't sure how he felt about it. Though mediation seemed to help Marlene articulate what she wanted, and had helped them come to an amicable agreement, he still thought he'd got the shorter end of the stick.

Marlene still had their life, most of their friends, and Chelsea. He had felt forced to leave and start over at a time in his life when he hadn't expected to be alone. Marlene was the one who chose to leave, forcing him to react, to make changes he didn't want to make.

"You should talk to Ahmed and make sure he or Annemarie can cover us for lunch. I'm planning to join you."

He glared at her. Did she think he needed someone to intervene in his conversations? He was nearly sixty, for heaven's sake. But then he softened. Betty had only his best interests in mind, and he had to give her the grace to do that. "I'll speak to Ahmed now. Then I'm going to go for a walk before we meet, if that's okay. I'll meet you at the Whisk. I just need to burn off some of this energy."

"Good idea," she said, looking a little relieved.

After squaring things with Ahmed, he walked down the street and toward the park that ran along the sea. Why did he let Raven's comments get to him? The mediator, when he met with her alone after settling the deal with

Marlene, suggested he might feel vulnerable now that he was leaving his old life. "You're leaving behind a long career where you were the expert, where you trained people, the whole works," the mediator had said. "This will be new. It may help to remind yourself that you have a lot of skills, that you ran a successful business."

"And failed at marriage," he said.

"You didn't fail. You grew. There is a difference. I see it a lot these days, you know. Men and women separating after twenty, thirty, even fifty years of marriage. It doesn't mean failure. It means you are growing into a different phase of your life."

"I never thought I would do it on my own."

"I know," she said. "Most don't see this in their future, especially after years together. But you have a plan. We've worked on it together. And it sounds pretty solid to me. I would love to try living in a new place, especially so close to the ocean."

"Well, if you're ever out my way, come on by the bookstore," he'd said. Though he hoped she wouldn't. He wanted to move on to his new life, and no matter what she said, he felt like a failure. He felt ashamed. And he felt anger, or at least defensiveness.

He kept walking, driving those feelings down again. Betty was right. He needed to stay calm. Stay curious, as the mediator had said. After their first meeting, Raven was probably feeling concerned too. She hadn't bargained on working with him. He was sure about that.

He walked for another half hour and then headed toward the bistro, stepping through the door at eleven forty-five. Then he heard the whir of the automatic door behind him. Betty had just arrived.

"Did you just get here too?" she asked, surveying the room. "Raven texted to say she would be a few minutes late."

"Is that a pattern I should expect?"

"Let's just say that Raven lives on island time. She grew up on one of the smaller islands, on one of the old communes that used to be out there."

"Communes?"

"I'll tell you later. Right now, I think we should join Curtis. He's the one near the counter. The one with the plaid shirt." Lance waited for Betty to lead the way.

Curtis shook their hands, and soon the two men fell into easy conversation. Curtis was a carpenter by trade, but because of an injury on the worksite, he was now doing less physical work by running the Men's Shack.

"It was a bit of a transition," admitted Curtis, "but it turned out to have a silver lining. As soon as my injuries were healed as well as expected, my wife was diagnosed with cancer. We had two good years together, though, before she passed on. If I hadn't been home with my injury and working with the city to get the Shack up and running, we wouldn't have had as much time together.

"And then, when I needed it most, the guys at the Shack were there to help me and my boys through."

"Curtis is also a musician," said Betty. "He and Rob Hudson, the man who runs the music store next door, started a band a few years ago."

"Nice," said Lance.

"We don't play many gigs except around town for festivals and such. But we have an annual fundraiser we put on."

"It's nice how everyone helps everyone else out," said Betty, and Lance nearly groaned. She was trying too hard to show him how well everyone got along and how much support was available. Hopefully she would ease off soon, spend less time at the store, and let him get on with things. Meanwhile he would have patience, though Marlene had always taken pains to point out that his patience wouldn't fill a bottle cap.

"Do you play an instrument?" asked Curtis.

"No, not unless you count the pipes I used to bang on," said Lance. "I'm more suited to being an appreciative audience."

"We can always use more of that," said Curtis. He looked up. "Hi, Raven, come join us."

Lance found Raven standing nearby and wondered how long she had been there. He'd been enjoying the conversation with Curtis, especially when he told him all about the Shack. Curtis was passionate about his work, and his crew had completed several projects, large and small, all over town. He had a group of regular workers as well as some who, with the Shack's support, were getting hours for their apprenticeships. It was clear Curtis had what it took to create the space for the cats in his window.

Raven sat down beside Lance. He shifted away a little to give her room.

"I see you've met," said Raven, unnecessarily. "Were you able to talk about the project at all? I brought the latest drawing of what we spoke about. She pulled a tube out of her tote bag and smoothed out a piece of paper on the table.

"Perfect," said Curtis. "We did talk about what you had in mind, but this helps a lot. What do you think, Lance?"

Lance looked at the three-dimensional drawing and couldn't help but be impressed. It was as good as many he'd seen drawn by professionals. "This helps me picture what you're talking about. Thanks." He smiled at Raven, and she smiled in return. They might work well together after all.

"One of the guys at the Shack wants to create the cat bed for you," said Curtis "It could go there." He pointed to a spot under a shelf. "The front would be removable for deep cleaning. Here, I'll show you the sketch."

He pulled out a drawing showing a circle with ears that would be the entrance for the cat bed. It was whimsical, and Lance liked it. Whimsy fit with what Pinky had set up on the very popular top floor, and he didn't want to mess with a good thing.

"There's a painting in the bookstore that would go with it," said Betty. "We could see if the artist could create one that would fit in the space." Then she stopped. "If you think that would be okay, Lance?"

He nearly barked with laughter. She was having a hard time letting go and couldn't help but stick her oar in. "I like that idea. Show me the painting you're thinking of when we get back."

"Of course." She smiled.

"When would you like to do the work?" Raven asked. "And how long do you think it will take?"

"We thought we'd put the pieces together at the Shack, and then it will probably take about an hour or two, tops, to assemble it. We can also paint the backdrop and around the inside windows for you. Raven mentioned that she and Betty had spoken about adding that on."

"That would help," said Betty. "The wood around those windows hasn't been painted in a few years, and fresh paint would make it easier to keep clean."

"We can complete the pieces this week and then come in to paint on Sunday after you close. If you remove everything from the other window, we can paint the display area on that one as well, so they match. Are you still closed on Mondays?"

They all turned to Lance. "For now, yes," he said. "I notice a lot of the street is closed on Mondays."

"In the summer, or on long weekends, we have sometimes opened," said Betty, "but I always enjoyed having Sunday after four until nine thirty on Tuesday available. It gave me time to do other things."

"We can come next Sunday after closing to do the painting. It shouldn't take more than two hours to tape and add two coats. Then we'd assemble the cat display on Monday afternoon once everything's dry. Raven, you can probably introduce a cat about a week after that."

"That sounds great," said Raven. "What do you think, Lance?"

"It's a good plan. We can set up the window next week, and meanwhile discuss how our processes will work," he said to Raven. She smiled one of those half smiles Marlene used to use when she wanted to look like she agreed. But deep down, he knew he had stepped in something. "I have some marketing help as well," he added, trying to help, but now she was clearly upset about something, so instead he changed the subject. "Okay." He rubbed his hands together. "Let's seal the deal with some lunch. Where do we go to order?"

They all put in their orders and spent a pleasant forty minutes talking about the Shack and about Betty's retirement plans, which sounded busier than Lance's regular work life. When they were done, Lance and Betty made their way back to the store to relieve Ahmed and Annemarie for lunch.

"Do you feel okay with this plan now?" asked Betty.

"I'm sure it will be fine." He liked Curtis and was confident in his experience managing projects. He was sure the work would be of good quality, but he still wasn't sure about Raven.

"They are a good bunch," said Betty. "Once you get to know them. It just takes time to fit into a new place."

"Good to know." He turned to help a customer who was looking for a book that had been discussed that morning on the radio. "Yes, I believe we have that one," he said, leading them to the Canadian section. The customer left with that title and another by the same author, and Lance felt great about how easily he was falling back into the routine he had learned as a teen. At least this part of his life plan was going okay.

He enjoyed reading, talking about books, and helping others find a good read. He looked up at the shelf near the back of the cash register and saw Rhett Butler staring down at him.

"And, yes, I'm in such a good mood I don't even mind you," he said to the cat. Then he caught Betty smiling at him from the end of an aisle.

"Just as long as you keep your distance," he added to the cat, and Rhett simply closed its eyes and settled in for a nap.

CHAPTER 9

*R*aven came away from lunch at the Whisk in a foul mood, angry at herself for once again being late. As usual, she had tried to cram too many errands into too little time and could hear her mother's voice reprimanding her for it even after all these years. "You have such a terrible concept of time," her mother said often. "You need to do better, Raven, if you're going to succeed in the regular world."

Thank goodness Curtis arrived on time to represent the project. He'd done a good job of connecting with Lance, especially considering he'd only received her last email the night before. But it still irked her that Lance had inserted himself into the meeting. He should have waited. He should have let them come to him with a fully formed plan. He… He…

Sigh.

It was true that he should not have been there, but it was also true that she should have said no when he asked to come. But how could she have done that? He had a way of getting what he wanted. His presence alone demanded that he be noticed. His voice was strong and demanding. He was demanding.

He took over the room just like Duane used to do. She frowned. Why was she thinking about Duane? She hadn't thought about him since her daughter's high school graduation, which he'd insisted on attending even though he hadn't visited for two years before that. And then he brought his new wife, Portia, who stood out like a shiny new penny. But at least Portia had been an ally when Duane started taking over the conversation at dinner that evening. Between the two of them, they managed to keep him under control until the meal was over and Wren went off with her friends to celebrate at a house party.

Lance reminded her of Duane. He couldn't let things go or trust that she and Curtis had things under control. Why did he have to run the Pages and Paws idea past his marketing consultant? Why did he want to consult on brand colors? Why did he need to bring in experts when she and Betty had already agreed that her approach and ideas were fine? She would have to find someone to bring her website into the twenties before he looked too closely at it, or he would have something to critique about that, too.

She climbed into her car and started the engine, prepared to head home, but then she glanced at the bag on the seat beside her. Groaning, she turned off the car and climbed out, taking the bag with her.

She walked past Making Sweet Music and down to a local clothing store that housed a tailor that a friend had recommended. As she stood at the back counter waiting for the tailor to finish measuring an older man for a suit, she started stewing again.

If she hadn't added, get new curtains to her earlier errand list, she would have been there on time. Now here she was, still trying to come up with a solution.

"Can I help you?" The tailor asked after finishing with his most recent customer.

"I hope so," she said. "I need a pair of curtains made, and I'm wondering if you could do it for me."

"I don't usually do that sort of thing," he said. "Especially this time of year. Wedding season is starting up."

"Do you know anyone who does?"

"Did you try the fabric store?"

"They sent me to you."

He shook his head. "I'm sorry for the wasted trip. Who did you speak to? I can't believe Gemma wouldn't have a better option."

"Thanks anyway," she said, and left the store discouraged. The fabric store was only a block away, so she walked back to it and asked to speak to Gemma.

Gemma, a woman of about forty-five, came to the counter, relieving the younger woman who had helped Raven pick fabric earlier that day. She explained the problem and what the tailor had said.

"I'm sorry, my staff is new. I'll have to talk to them about where they send people in the future. But for your problem, I can suggest only two options. One is to find a home sewer who can help, though this time of year anyone who takes on clients is sewing costumes for the dance or gymnastics studio or graduation. I have a list of phone numbers in the back, but it may take a few weeks."

"Okay. You said that was one option. What's the other one?"

"Learning to sew them yourself. I run a class for drop-in sewers who need a bit of guidance—or sometimes they just need to use a machine. I take everyone from beginners to those learning to tailor."

"'When is this class?"

"I have classes on Tuesday and Thursday evenings. They run from seven to nine, and you can sign up either here or online."

"How long would it take for me to make a pair of curtains?" Raven reached into the shopping bag and pulled out the curtain from Lance's camper.

Gemma took the fabric and examined it. "This shouldn't be too difficult."

"I took wood shop in high school, so I have little experience sewing besides darning socks, hand-sewing a patch, or fixing a hem. I've never operated a sewing machine."

"Well, it would probably take two classes—possibly three, but that's not likely. The curtains are small, so it's not a lot of sewing time. You would need to measure them, cut the fabric, and I would show you how to run the machine the first day. Give you time to practice. Then the next day you could probably finish it."

"When's the first class?"

"I'm full tonight, but I have space on Thursday night," said Gemma, scanning the computer screen. "And Tuesday as well."

Raven pulled her phone out of her pocket and scrolled through her calendar. She had help at the sanctuary both those days. She would've preferred to stay home with a good book and help Sebastien get used to the house, but she needed to fix this mess first.

"Sign me up," she said, giving Gemma her name and contact information and handing over her credit card. She had never felt the need to learn to sew, but if her sister, who made all her own clothes, had figured out how to do it, she could too.

She walked back to her car, happy that she'd found a solution to her curtain problem. Once she gave Lance his new curtains, she would feel better, and maybe he would see her as reliable—as someone who fixed her own messes.

Yes. Everything would to be just fine. He was new. They got off to a rocky start. But if she gave him new curtains and proved that she, too, kept her word, their relationship might improve. She opened her car door and slid behind the wheel. Next stop, the market.

As she shifted the car into drive, she noticed a piece of paper under her windshield wiper. Why did people need to put advertising flyers on cars? She got out of the car and grabbed it, then settled back in her seat, cursing under her breath when she read the paper. It wasn't a flyer. It was a parking ticket. And though deep down she knew she was overreacting and misdirecting her anger, she blamed Lance Reed for it one hundred percent.

Since arriving in town, the man had done nothing but upend her life, and if it weren't for her need to work with him on this project, she would love never to see him again.

But as things stood, she was now going to go home and spend a lot of time picking out the best cat she had to introduce to the bookstore in two weeks. She could not afford to make another mistake if she wanted this partnership to get on track.

CHAPTER 10

By the end of the day on Tuesday, Lance was tired of learning new things and smiling at customers. Betty had left around three to go to a physiotherapy appointment, and he closed up, walked the two blocks to the bank to make his deposit, and walked back to the store. All he wanted to do was straighten up the front display, go to his apartment with some takeaway food, and veg in front of the television. He didn't even have the energy to read the next book in the fantasy series he was reading.

He took out a table he used as a TV tray and set it in front of his favorite chair, the one he'd dragged all the way across Canada. It fit like a comfortable old shoe, and today he needed something comfortable.

He was about to sit and eat the decaf coffee and sandwich he'd purchased when he saw something move near the couch. Mice? He shouldn't have mice, unless Betty had exaggerated Rhett Butler's mousing abilities.

He waited for movement. Seeing nothing, he took another bite of his sandwich and reached for the remote. Then he heard something. Quickly he put the TV on mute and turned toward the direction of the noise.

Mrowww.

"What are you doing here?" Rhett Butler had moved from wherever he was hiding to sit on the sofa.

Mrowww, the cat answered then licked his chops and stared at Lance's sandwich.

"Didn't you get dinner?"

Mrowww. The cat was louder now.

"Fine," said Lance, looking at the sandwich and then back at the cat. "You can have a piece of chicken."

As though understanding him, Rhett Butler dropped to the floor and walked over to Lance's chair, where he sat looking up at him expectantly.

"Do you think if you beg like a dog, I will like you better?"

The cat sat, his eyes trained on the sandwich, until Lance relented. "Okay. You can have a bit of the chicken, but I'm sure you got fed today." He took a piece of chicken out of the sandwich and handed it to the cat.

Rhett Butler took it slowly, placed it on the ground, and ate it bite by bite, like the gentleman he was. Then he stood, blinked at Lance, hopped back on the sofa, curled up, and closed his eyes.

"You can't stay here," said Lance. "I don't like cats."

But the only response was the loud purr of a contented cat.

"Well, maybe you can stay for one night," said Lance, before picking up his coffee and turning the volume up on the thriller he found on television. "But tomorrow, you're going to have to stay in the store."

But Rhett didn't stay in the store the next night, or the night after that. It soon became a ritual. Lance would turn the closed sign around, walk to the office, get the deposit ready, and Rhett would wait for him at the door to the apartment.

Lance would let him in, go for a walk to deposit the day's receipts, pick up a takeout meal, and walk home.

When he got back to the apartment, he would serve Rhett a small meal of cat food in the extra dish he'd purchased, or he would share some of his food with the cat.

Then Rhett would curl up on the sofa until Lance went to bed when he would follow him into the room and sleep in the corner.

Lance appreciated the cat's presence. After months of being alone in the family home and on the road west, it was comforting to have another heartbeat in the house. Because no matter how amicable his divorce or how smooth his transition to his new life, he still had one big problem.

How to deal with the loneliness.

By Sunday, Lance had a better handle on things. He'd adapted to the store schedule, to the number of customers who came in, and he understood who the suppliers were, when and how to order stock, how and where to file government forms, and even how to read and analyze Betty's many spreadsheets.

When the Shack project group showed up to paint that afternoon, he found he had enough energy to talk to Curtis, who came to supervise a pair of younger men, and to find out more about the various happenings in town. They sat at the counter, each with a bottle of kombucha Curtis had brought along, and Curtis shared his ideas of where to catch trout and which restaurants to try first, as Lance was tired of chicken sandwiches. Even Rhett Butler had turned up his nose at it the night before.

"There's a farmers market down by the pier on Wednesdays from about eleven to three. It runs from May to October every year, and that's where I go for my vegetables. Otherwise, I go up to the other end of town. It's less expensive," said Curtis.

"I'll have to explore that end of town tomorrow morning. What time do you plan on coming in?"

"I talked to Raven. She asked if we could meet about three. She's got a fair amount of work to do at the sanctuary, and people pick up their cats on Monday mornings."

"How long have you known Raven?"

"We went to high school together at the north end of the island. Then I went to trade school, and she went to university for a degree in business management."

"Business management?"

Curtis laughed. "You wouldn't know it, but she's got serious skills. She ran her ex-husband's software business, and they made a killing when they sold it. She also ran a hardware store for a few years at the other end of town, until she tired of the commute and she and Rosalyn decided to take in cats."

"But how does she make money taking in cats?"

"I don't think she needs it," Curtis said, taking a pull on his drink. "She ran the hardware store for a friend who needed help while she got cancer treatment. From what I know, she made the store much more profitable in the two years she ran it. Her friend can't say enough about her."

"Betty said she grew up on a commune."

"Not a commune," said Curtis. "A tiny island with just her parents, her sister, and a couple of other families. They lived off the land, fishing and farming, and then in the eighties her parents began putting together kits— like hydroponics and stuff to do with growing herbs—

and sold them through the mail. Now they sell online, and their cousin runs it, but I think Raven and her sister Drew still have shares in the business."

"So, she's a tycoon?"

"She wouldn't see herself like that. She's just an animal person trying to deal with the boom in the kitten population. And she loves it. Don't let her tell you otherwise. Though I think she gets lonely sometimes since Wren left. Not sure what I'll do when my youngest son leaves home. Hopefully I'll be able to deal with it as well as Raven does."

"Maybe she'll find a partner," Lance mused.

"Doubt it. Her ex, from what I've seen, ruined her for other guys. Rave's been on her own for a dozen years, and I think she likes it that way. I wouldn't waste my time if I were you."

"Oh, no," said Lance, horrified. "Not me. I've only been divorced five months," he said, "I'm not looking for a relationship right now."

"I understand. It's taken me a few years to come to terms with my wife's death, and moving on when you have a teen is hard to do."

"It's hard to do even if you don't have a teen."

They turned the conversation to other topics and spent a pleasant hour while the crew taped and painted the windows.

When the guys were done, Curtis and Lance walked over to inspect the work. "Looks great," said Lance. "The color you chose really brightens up the place."

"Oh, that's all Raven," said Curtis. "She's the one with the vision. I just follow directions."

"Well, it looks great," he said again. Though his thoughts strayed to another accomplished woman with vision when it came to renovations. Marlene needed no one. Especially him. No matter how attractive he found Raven to be, he needed to steer clear, or he would risk repeating past mistakes.

He said his goodbyes and locked the door, promising to be there at three the next day to let them in and finish the work. Then he turned to find Rhett Butler waiting for him at the door to their shared home.

He sighed. Maybe he and his furry friend would be better off alone.

CHAPTER 11

*R*aven arrived at three to meet Curtis and stepped across the threshold of the store, expecting to be shuffled off to the side while Lance took over.

He greeted her, then said, "I've got a few things to do out back. I'll see you later."

"You don't want to supervise?" she asked, with an edge to her voice.

He raised his eyebrows at her, and Curtis swiveled around to stare in her direction.

"I trust you," said Lance. He turned to Curtis. "I'll be back in a while with something to drink. Is iced tea okay?"

"Sounds great," said Curtis, turning to help the crew start assembling the display.

Raven watched them work for a few minutes until Curtis walked over to join her. "Do you need me here?" she asked.

"Thought you'd like to see how it turned out," he said. "Didn't realize you have an issue with Lance, or I wouldn't have suggested you come in."

"I don't have an issue with him."

"No? You sure fooled me. Hang on a second." He went back to the crew near the window to answer a question, then returned to Raven.

"Well?" he said.

She frowned. "I find him kind of pushy."

"Really? I haven't noticed that about him."

"Well, you're a guy. He doesn't take over when you're around. Didn't you see how he behaved at our meeting the other day?"

"I just remember him asking questions, trying to understand what we were going to do to his store. He's new to town and not so used to small-town living. You should give the guy a break."

"I'll try," she said. "But he doesn't even like cats."

"That store cat likes him. Follows him everywhere."

She scanned the room for Rhett Butler, but couldn't locate him. "I'll have to take your word on that."

"I've never seen you so bothered by a man before," said Curtis. "If I didn't know better, I'd think you had a thing for him."

"It's a good thing you know better, then," she said. "Listen, I have a small errand to run. Can you do without me for a bit?"

"Sure," said Curtis, laughing. "You sure you aren't making an excuse to avoid my questions? Am I getting too close to the truth?"

"Shut it," she whispered so the others wouldn't hear. Then she pushed the front door, which didn't budge. Curtis was laughing louder now as she fumbled to unlock it, and she was relieved when it finally swung open and allowed her to escape. Sometimes friends could be so infuriating.

She hastened down the street to her hatchback, which she'd parked in front of the fabric shop, and pulled out her mother's old sewing machine in its equally old carrying case. She lugged it the few quick steps to the store.

Gemma sat with a circle of women, showing them all how to smock. Her face lit up when Raven walked in, and she excused herself.

"Let's take a look," she said, and helped Raven lift the machine to the counter.

"It's been sitting in the back room of my house since my sister handed it down to me. She got a new one, all computerized and fancy, and dropped Mom's old machine off one day. She's been after me for years to try sewing."

"So, you enjoyed your first lesson?" said Gemma, looking over the machine.

"Surprisingly, yes. I've always avoided sewing, though I did like sewing patches on my jeans and doing a bit of embroidery. I'm hoping the machine still works. Thanks for letting me bring it in."

"No problem. The technician is coming in tomorrow, and I often add an extra machine or two for him to service while he's here. The fee will be nominal compared to taking it down to Victoria." She unpacked the machine and set it on a table near a line of others. "You're sure it still runs?"

"Yes. Drew, my sister, said it just needs to be oiled and tuned and whatnot."

"Provided the tech finds nothing wrong with it, I can show you how to use it when you come in tomorrow night, and you can finish the curtains on your own machine."

"That would be fantastic," said Raven. "To tell you the truth, I always avoided sewing because it was Drew's thing. She makes beautiful clothes and makes it seem so easy. Like with everything she tries. I figured I wouldn't do nearly as well compared to her."

"Comparison-itis is a dangerous disease," said Gemma. "A lot of my students come in with stories of other, more creative people in their lives, but then they realize there is as much joy in the process of creating things as in using the finished product. Did you see some of the work that lot is doing?" She nodded toward the sewing circle. "None of them knew the first thing about smocking three weeks ago."

"I saw some of the samples as I walked by," said Raven. "You are a good teacher."

Gemma laughed. "I can't take the credit. I just encourage the creative spirit in my students to come out and play. And now that the sewing bug bit you, you'll need to decide what else you'd like to try."

"I already know," said Raven, pointing to a quilt on the wall. It showed a bald eagle with a salmon in its talons. "I want to learn to quilt. Something with cats that's small to start."

"If you have a few minutes, you can look at the patterns." She pointed toward a stand that held quilting patterns. "I have several beginner cat patterns that would make a nice cushion cover or wall hanging."

Raven thanked her new friend and went over to the wall to peruse the patterns. She chose a booklet with three different options and took it to the counter.

"Good choice," said Gemma as she rang up the sale. "And tomorrow, if you come in a little before class, I can help you find fabric for it. Some of these would only need a couple of fat quarters or inexpensive remnants."

"Thank you," said Raven, paying for the pattern and slipping it into her tote bag. "I'll see you tomorrow."

Raven walked back to the bookstore, happy with her purchase and proud of herself for trying something new. She glanced at her watch and discovered she'd been gone an hour. Hopefully the crew had finished their work and Curtis had forgotten his embarrassing line of questioning.

She didn't want to talk about Lance and feelings in the same sentence. And she especially didn't want to know why he bothered her so much.

As she passed the display window, she saw that the pieces were all in place, including the Pages and Paws backdrop she had designed and ordered. She hoped Mr. Can't-Be-Pleased would like the signage. The cost was minimal, but she had spent several hours working with a graphic designer friend to get it right.

"Hey, you're just in time," said Curtis as she pushed at the door and found it still unlocked.

"It looks great from outside."

"Look at it from this angle," he said, stepping back and swinging open the back panel. "We put in a small door you can latch or unlatch from the outside. It's the easy way to let the cats in and out. And we put the litter box under that first shelf so it can't be seen from the window." Raven smiled and listened as he continued to point out all the details.

Curtis got excited about his projects when he added details people didn't expect. On any normal day she would be just as excited—his enthusiasm was that infectious. Today, however, when Lance walked toward them, all she could do was watch for his reaction. She hoped he would be happy with her design now that it was installed.

Lance stopped beside the front window and listened patiently as Curtis repeated everything he told Raven, and her relief was palpable when he smiled and said it looked even better than it had on paper.

"When would you like to start with the cats?" she asked, ignoring the small wince around his eyes.

"Let's decide next week, after we discuss marketing and processes. My daughter and her friend, who has some experience marketing not-for-profits and building websites, are coming this weekend. They promised to give me some ideas."

She frowned. Why did he need anyone else involved?

"They're the demographic I want to attract to the store," he said, as though expecting her question. "Early to late twenties."

"That makes sense," she said, surprised he'd thought of it. Maybe bringing someone else in would help. She only had access to younger people through the women who worked for her, and they weren't the target demographic since they already had access to cats.

"It also gives me an opportunity to visit with my daughter," he said. "She's been living in Vancouver for close to four years, and I have seen little of her since she moved out here for school. Are you around this weekend? Can I bring her out to visit the cats?"

"Yes, absolutely. Her friend wouldn't happen to know how to hook up a webcam, would she?"

"I think it's a he," said Lance. "And I am not sure of his skills in that department. But I can ask."

"One of the guys at the Shack may know," said Curtis, who was listening to their exchange.

"That might be the better bet," said Lance. "We might need someone local in case we have any technical difficulty."

"That's true," said Raven, with a small amount of appreciation. He may like to take over, but at least he was detail-oriented enough to think of things she hadn't considered yet.

"I'll ask the guys and let you know," said Curtis.

After cleaning up the materials and tools and sweeping the sawdust off the floor, Curtis and the crew left the store. Raven stayed behind a moment to ask Lance what Zoey and her friend would need to help build a marketing plan, and she left with a better view of Lance now that she understood his motivation for bringing in help.

As she slid into her car, she tamped down the niggling feeling that there was another reason she was happy that Lance was different than she'd first thought. She would ignore that feeling because self-reflection, to her mind, opened a person up to thoughts and ideas that were better left buried. Self-knowledge, especially when it came to her and the opposite sex, was a highly overrated concept.

CHAPTER 12

*O*n Friday after closing, Lance stood outside the ferry terminal waiting for Zoey, relieved she'd agreed to come—even if Axel was tagging along.

"He has tons of experience providing marketing and communications for not-for-profits," she said. "And he's super excited to help."

Tempting her with the opportunity to spend time with kittens hadn't hurt either. Zoey had always wanted one, but he'd always deterred his girls from having pets.

Besides, he wanted to check out this Axel character. While Zoey, as Marlene often told him, was a grown woman who could engage in relationships with anyone she chose, Lance couldn't help being protective. After all, he had been protecting her his whole life. It was a difficult habit to let go.

"Hey, Dad!" He turned and waved at Zoey. To his relief, she was dressed in jeans, a T-shirt, and a light jacket rather than the smart, professional outfit she'd worn a week earlier. This was the Zoey he watched hockey games with. The one he knew.

She hugged him and turned back toward the man walking beside her. "Dad, this is my friend Axel. Can you believe he's lived in Vancouver six years and has never been to the island?"

"Axel," said Lance, holding out his hand. Zoey's friend was tall and slim, with dark-rimmed glasses and a shock of dark-brown hair. He was also older than any of Zoey's previous boyfriends. Though, Lance reminded himself, boys grew quite a bit between seventeen and twenty-five, and the last time she'd introduced him to a boyfriend, it was before her high school graduation dance.

Axel shook his hand. "Nice to meet you, sir." His tone was polite and his handshake firm. Two things in his favor, though Lance didn't much like being called *sir*.

"Call me Lance," he said, guiding them back toward the truck. "Come, I'll take you home to drop off your stuff. Are you hungry at all? Do you like Indian food?"

"Love Indian food," said Axel.

Another point in his favor.

"Great. There's a place down by the boardwalk I've wanted to try." They walked to the truck and squeezed into the front bench seat, with Zoey in the middle.

"Tomorrow I have to open the store at nine, but once my staff arrive at ten, I can take you out to see some sights. Or I can give you the keys to the truck if you remember how to drive a stick," he said.

"We don't need to go without you. We'll wait," said Zoey. "And of course I can still drive this old thing, though I'm surprised it made it all the way across Canada."

"Hey! Don't mock my truck."

She laughed. "I—" She looked at Axel. "I mean *we* thought we should tour the store before we go out to meet your new partner."

"Partner?"

"Isn't that what the cat woman is? A partner?"

"I suppose in this initiative," said Lance, though "partner" was stretching things a bit.

"I can't wait to see the cats. Then we can discuss your websites and approach. We reviewed both your sites on the trip over and have some ideas to help streamline processes."

"Zoey," said Axel. "We just got here, and you're already working."

"A family fault, I'm afraid," said Lance as he turned onto the street toward town. "We're a family of workaholics."

Axel laughed. "Well, now I understand where it comes from."

"You're no better," said Zoey, elbowing him in the side. "Who's the first one in to work and the last one out every day?"

"That's different," he said, though Lance heard the smile in his voice. Gainful employment was another point in the man's favor. And he knew his daughter well and had a sense of humor. So far, six out of six. If he wasn't careful, he might really like this guy.

"Have you heard from Chelsea?" asked Zoey.

"I spoke with her on Monday and told her about the store and the new project. She laughed because of how much I dislike felines."

"I have to say I had a giggle myself," said Zoey. "How are you going to do it?"

"I figure it's only two cats at a time. Plus, Rhett Butler, the store cat. And the staff are excited to help care for them. My job is to avoid getting involved and mind my step."

Zoey chuckled. "Rhett Butler. That's a funny name."

"He's a tuxedo cat. Betty named him. It's a character from *Gone with the Wind*."

"*Gone with the Wind*?"

"American classic. The character is a southern gentleman with an attitude."

"Oh, so she named him after a gentleman because of the tuxedo. That makes sense. But you may end up getting more involved than you think. Cats have a way of doing what they want, where they want."

"Aunt Betty made the deal, so I can't go back on it, and right now it's a six-month experiment. I can put up with a lot of things for six months." He finished renovating his empty family house for six months, erasing memories and dreams that took a lifetime to build. This would be a mere inconvenience by comparison.

"Did Chelsea say anything when she called?"

"Just the usual." Lance glanced over his left shoulder and merged the truck onto the main road. "She's working in admissions at the hospital for the summer. She's excited about it."

"Hmm."

"Why do you ask? Is something up?"

"No. Nothing. I haven't talked to her for a few days, that's all," she said a little too quickly. He would have pressed her, but as they approached First Avenue, they entered thicker traffic, so he said nothing further until he pulled the truck up behind the store.

"We're here. Let's put your gear upstairs, and then we can walk over to the restaurant."

They climbed the stairs to the three-bedroom apartment

above the store. "It's not bad," said Zoey. "You need to do some painting and updates, but it's got good bones."

"You sound like your mother," said Lance. And, unlike months ago, there was no lump in his throat when he mentioned Marlene. The loss had gone from something unbearable to something he didn't think about as often.

He turned toward Axel. "Zoey's mother is always looking at older houses and coming up with ways to update them. I suppose that's why she went into real estate."

"Mom has a talent for picturing possibilities," said Zoey. "But Dad is the one who did the work to make her vision a reality. How many houses did you and Mom redo, Dad?"

"Including our last one? Fourteen. Though we lived in the last one for about ten years. Here, I'll give you a quick tour." He showed them to the guest rooms. One had a bed and side tables, and the second had a desk and a fold-out couch, which he'd made up already. Both rooms had televisions and bookshelves that still needed to be filled. But the quilts and throw pillows Betty had left for him made the rooms look less like an afterthought and more like a place someone might wish to visit again. He hoped so. He missed his daughters.

He continued the tour by showing them his room and the main living area.

"They designed the kitchen for Betty and her wheel-chair, so I'm going to redo it. In the meantime, I've been eating out a lot. At least that's my excuse." There were two counters he could use, likely made for his uncle when he was alive, but he hated cooking for one. "We can leave in a moment." He went to the cupboard to get a can of cat food and opened it onto a dish on the floor.

"What's that for?" asked Zoey.

"Rhett Butler hangs out with me in the evenings." And, right on cue, Rhett walked up to the dish and settled down to eat his meal.

"Oh, he's so handsome!" said Zoey. "I can't believe you have a cat, Dad."

"I can't either," said Lance, giving the cat a quick scratch behind the ears.

After Axel put his bag in the guest room and Zoey took the room with the fold-out couch, he suggested they walk to the restaurant. For the rest of the evening he played tour guide, answering questions about the island whenever he could and talking about all the places where he spent time as a child.

"You came here a lot when you were young?" asked Zoey.

"My father moved out here after his divorce. He always worked in camps in the oil fields, so I would stay with Betty a lot of the summer, help her in the store, and explore the island with my uncle, and with Dad when he was home."

"And this is where you met Uncle Del?"

"Yes." He smiled at the memories. "Del and I used to explore together. And when he turned sixteen and got a driver's license, we started going down the island to fish for salmon every year. We still go fishing as often as we can. Tradition."

"Maybe one day we can go with you," said Zoey. "Axel fishes."

"Haven't for a few years," said Axel. "I grew up in Alberta, so mostly lake and river trout."

"When I plan another salmon fishing trip, I'll let you know," said Lance. He glanced at Axel through his peripheral vision and noticed the grin.

Yes, Axel was growing on him by the minute, and he was okay with that.

The next morning, Lance showed them around the store while Zoey made notes on a tablet. When the weekend staff arrived, they piled into the truck and headed out to Raven's place.

Axel let out a soft whistle as they pulled up the driveway. "Wow. Nice property."

"They keep the cats in that section off the main house." Lance pulled the truck into the driveway and pointed toward the building.

"This is such a fabulous place," said Zoey. She slid out of the truck and onto the gravel path. "But what do they do for fun?"

"Are you kidding?" Axel said. "I bet there are great hiking trails, places to camp. Can you imagine sitting out there?" He pointed to the verandah off the second house. "I could spend the whole day out there reading."

Zoey cocked her head and peered up at him. "You sound like him," she said, pointing her chin toward Lance. Then she laughed, as though to cover up the realization that she was attracted to a man like her father. "Though it would be a great place to kick back after work."

"And for a barbecue," said Axel. "And look, Zoey—" He pulled her away to show her another feature he'd noticed, but Lance didn't follow. Instead, he turned toward the footsteps crunching in the gravel driveway and caught his breath.

Raven's hair was down today. Instead of the severe ponytail or bun she'd worn during their past encounters, her black hair fell in soft curls that framed her face and hung well past her shoulders. She seemed less worried and uptight than before. Something else was different about her, too, and it took him a moment to figure out what it was. Her smile. It wasn't the strained, polite half smile she'd used with him in the past. This one was real. As though she was glad to see him.

Which was good because, for reasons he didn't want to examine too closely, he was certainly glad to see her.

She stopped in front of him and shook his hand. "Thanks for coming. I'm afraid I have a couple of kittens to feed before we can start. One of my staff is sick this morning. Though," she said in a low voice, "I suspect it's the twenty-six-ounce flu, and completely self-inflicted. It was her nineteenth birthday yesterday."

Lance laughed. "We've all been there. I think it may have been my nineteenth birthday bash that cured me of any need to overindulge again."

Raven smiled her lovely smile again, and he felt his pulse quicken a little. She really was attractive, even in sweatpants and knee-high gumboots.

"You brought your consultants?" She frowned a little at the pair standing nearby, teasing each other like high school students, and he realized they probably appeared less accomplished than he knew them to be.

"Zoey, Axel, come and meet Raven," he said. The pair turned around, and his daughter's eyes widened while Axel quickly schooled his features into a professional expression. He walked over and stuck out his hand to shake Raven's, while she turned her warm smile on them.

"Zoey and Axel have done quite a bit of work to prepare for this meeting," he said. "They've got questions about how we plan to take applications, contact applicants, et cetera. And I've asked them to update my website so we can take applications online as well as at the store. It will help during busy times if we have a place to direct anyone who wants more information."

"Thanks for meeting us," said Axel, taking over the lead in the conversation. He introduced himself and talked about their preparations, which had included an audit of the websites for both businesses and a perusal of the bookstore. To Lance's surprise, he and Zoey had even gone out to explore a bookstore on the mainland that also put cats in their windows, to learn how they did it.

"There was a great restaurant nearby," said Zoey to her father. "I kept the receipt so I can add it to our invoice."

Lance chuckled. "Well, if it only costs me dinner and you got some great intel, it sounds like a deal."

"It's unnecessary, sir... Lance," Axel said. "We also went to play paintball with some friends, so it was on our way." He frowned at Zoey, who just laughed. "Can we see where you keep the cats, then map out the process you're going to use to link them to their new homes?"

"This way." Raven led them to the end of the house Lance hadn't seen before.

"What is that building going to be?" asked Axel, pointing to the half-built structure.

"That's a new expansion. But until I can fund it, it remains in the lockup phase."

"Is it part of the nonprofit arm?"

"It's complicated," said Raven. "I have a cat kennel, which I will show you first. It funds the cat sanctuary. I want to use that new building to board more cats and about twenty dogs."

"You mean that the rescue part is something you do for free?"

"Until about five years ago, we only ever had one or two at a time. But since the pandemic—and for reasons that elude me—people are giving up their cats at a faster rate. So now I have about fifteen rescues and only ten spots for the kennel. It's why I needed to find another way to showcase them."

"I'm sure you could make this into a not-for-profit and encourage donations," Axel said. "I can explore what it might take to do that if you like."

"No need. I have a friend; she is a vet. Rosalyn and I have been doing this for years, and she used to have most of her practice out here. So, until about a year ago, except for a handful of cats, this was a business. She's working on the paperwork to change it over." She opened the door. "Come on in."

They stepped into the building and came to a reception desk, where Lance recognized a familiar face.

"Hello again," said Mal. "How did your camping trip go?"

"Better, thanks to all your work," said Lance. "I think the camper is cleaner than it's been in years. Thank you."

"And Raven tells me you're the new owner of the bookstore." She smirked at Raven, and Raven immediately took over the conversation, giving him the sense that whatever Raven had told Mal, it hadn't been flattering.

"Axel and Zoey, this is Mal. She is my right-hand person. Daisy, who is unfortunately ill this morning, is my other full-time worker. They live next door."

"Nice digs," said Axel to Mal. "Zoey and I were just admiring your verandah and your view."

"It's a definite perk to the job," said Mal with a smile. "Which reminds me: I have to put the laundry into the dryer now, so please excuse me."

"When you're done with that, could you put these where they belong as well?" Raven took a small pile of fabric from under the counter and set it on top. "If you give her the keys to your camper," she said to Lance, "we can have them installed before you leave."

"What?" He looked at the fabric, which featured a man fishing from the shore and sailboats in the background.

"They are to replace the curtains that Sebastien and I destroyed," said Raven.

"Who's Sebastien?" asked Zoey, looking between him and Raven with a glint in her eye. What was she thinking?

"I'll introduce you to Sebastien in a few minutes," said Raven, but her eyes were still on him, waiting for his response.

"Where did you find them?" he asked. "They're perfect."

"I made them," she said. "It was easier than looking all over town or searching the internet."

"You made them?" He picked them up and unfolded the curtains. They were lined and made of two panels with similar scenes. "That is well above and beyond. I told you I would replace them," he said.

"And I like to keep my word," she said. "If you leave Mal the key to the camper, she can put them up for you."

Lance pulled his keys out of his pocket and set them down on the counter, then touched the curtains again. No one had sewed anything for him since Betty made him a quilt when he was a child. His heart squeezed a little at the enormity of the gift.

"Thank you," he said to Raven. "I love them."

Their eyes met for a moment, and she flushed a little. Then she said, "Come, let me show you the rest." And ushered them through a door to the cattery, which housed those cats being boarded.

"Over here is where Rosalyn examines the animals," said Raven, pushing open a door to an office with an examination table and shelves for vet supplies. "She still comes out here one day a week so she can be available for some of her rural customers."

Then she led them through another door to where the rescue cats lived. She pointed at an orange cat sitting in his pen, quietly grooming himself.

"You remember Sebastien."

"We meet again," said Lance, staying a safe distance away.

"This is the cat who ruined the curtains?" asked Zoey.

"Yes, he found his way into your dad's camper when he got away on the ferry," said Raven, and she told Zoey what happened.

Zoey hooted with laughter. "You know Dad hates cats?" she said. "Wait until I tell Chelsea. She's going to love this."

Lance frowned at his daughter, causing her to laugh again. "You have Sebastien in your home?"

"He's doing well. My cat has made him comfortable, and he's settled right down."

"You must have a magical touch," said Lance. "I didn't think he would ever calm down."

"They don't call me the cat whisperer for nothing." Raven smiled. "Come and see the other pair."

She took them out another door to a connecting breezeway that led to the main house.

"This is where I keep kittens and any cats that need extra recovery time. It's quieter and easier for me to access at night." She opened the pen holding the little gray kittens and picked up the closest one.

"Their ears are all perked up now," said Lance. "And their fur is much thicker."

"They're almost ready to come in the house," said Raven. "Would you like to help me feed them?" she asked Zoey.

Zoey's eyes lit up, and she reached out to take the kitten from Raven. "What are their names?"

"My staff and I have been tossing ideas around. We think, because we want to have them adopted through the bookstore, we would call them Dot and Dash. You know, like periods and hyphens in sentences."

She handed the second cat to Axel after demonstrating how to hold it, and gave them each a bottle of formula to feed the kittens.

"Hello, Dash," said Zoey. The tiny kitten mewled softly until it latched on to the nipple. "You were hungry."

"They are so tiny," said Axel, holding the kitten carefully as he fed it. "Are these the ones you want to put on the webcam?"

"Yes, I have it right over there on the shelf, but I haven't had time to learn how to hook it up so I can stream it to my computer."

"I can do that," said Axel. "I mean, if you would like some help. It won't take more that fifteen or twenty minutes."

"I would," said Raven. "And if you can show me how to stream it, that would be very helpful too. I was going to figure it out by watching YouTube videos, but I haven't had the time."

"I can do it after we talk about the adoption process," said Axel. "It would help if we can use what already works and just add things based on what is changing— before we rebuild Lance's website."

"Once we're done here, we should probably retire to my kitchen table. Do you two like chocolate chips?"

"You didn't," said Lance, his mouth already watering.

"Yes, I did." She laughed.

"You're going to have to visit your sister again soon," he said, "or give up the habit entirely."

Raven laughed, and Zoey looked between them, puzzled.

"Raven gets this great cookie dough from the mainland," said Lance. "You're going to love them."

"I can't wait," said Zoey. "Though you surprise me, Dad. First cats in the house and now chocolate chip cookies? I barely recognize you."

"Cats in the house?" asked Raven.

"Dad lets the store cat come home with him at night."

"In my defense, it was his home first. Betty has been letting him come home with her since he was a kitten. Didn't seem fair to make him change his ways. He's rather an old cat."

"That's sweet, Dad," said Zoey, giving him a little punch in his arm.

He grunted in response and was happy to leave the pair to feed the cats when Raven beckoned him to the other end of the room.

"I've been considering which of the cats we should start with, and I've settled on this one. She pointed toward a small tortoiseshell cat curled up asleep in a corner of her pen.

"This is T—"

"Turtle," he said, as a rush of memories he'd kept bottled up for decades flowed through his mind.

"No, Tilly," Raven said, a question in her voice.

"I'm… going to see if Mal needs anything from me. I'll be back in a few minutes." It was a flimsy excuse to get away from prying eyes, but he didn't escape before noticing the look Raven was giving him. *Please let me out of here before I embarrass myself.*

He walked outside intending to head down the driveway, but the clouds that had threatened all morning chose that moment to make good on their promise and opened their contents.

"Dammit," he muttered, increasing his pace until he reached the truck. He climbed inside the camper, slammed the door, and sat at the little table with his head in his hands.

Maybe looking after all these cats was a bad idea after all.

CHAPTER 13

*R*aven stared after him, her mouth open. What was wrong with the man? She glanced over to Zoey and Axel, who were still feeding kittens and chatting, oblivious to Lance's sudden departure. Too bad. She would have loved to ask Zoey if this was a regular occurrence. Now, she would have to ask him herself, because she had no patience for his mercurial moods. If he didn't want cats in his store, she needed to end this now.

"I'm just going to check on Mal to make sure the curtains got in okay. Once these two are done eating, could you put them back in their pen? And if I'm not back, perhaps you can look at that webcam?"

"Okay," said Zoey.

Raven barely heard her through the haze of anger building up inside. What made him think he could just walk out like that? She got to the doorway and looked out into the driving rain. Where was he?

"He went into the camper," said Mal, who was sitting behind the desk.

"Thanks," muttered Raven. She pulled her jacket collar up over her head, ran to the vehicle, and banged on the door.

"Yeah?"

Not waiting to be asked, she opened the door and climbed in, taking a seat across from him.

"What is this about?" she asked. "I've tried so hard to make sure I took all your specifications into consideration, and now you can't even look at the cat I chose."

"I'm sorry. It took me by surprise. I've never seen a cat that looked like Turtle before."

"Who is Turtle?"

"Turtle was my cat when I was a kid."

"And you didn't like the cat?"

"I loved that cat."

"I'm not following, Lance."

He sighed. "When I was a kid, my father worked in mining camps. Two weeks in, two weeks at home. When he was gone, it was just me and my mother at home in Toronto." He frowned. "I don't think I've told anyone about this. Other than Marlene."

She gazed at his downturned face, and her anger receded. He was obviously distraught. She waited for him to continue.

"One day Dad brought me a tortoiseshell cat exactly like the one you have inside."

"Tilly," she said.

"Yes. I had begged my dad for a pet, and what I really wanted was a turtle. I'd read quite a bit about them, and at first I was disappointed. So I named her Turtle." He smiled, and she chuckled and let herself breathe more deeply.

"My mother was an actress. Mostly plays, but she had some minor television appearances and commercials. She was good to me, but when there was an opportunity to pursue her dream, she often got tunnel vision. I learned early on to fend for myself when Dad was out of town, and I said nothing about her leaving me alone sometimes. Or about having to heat up my own TV dinners in the oven.

"The one time I told my father about being left, they had an awful fight and I retreated to my room. It's probably why I love reading so much. I was a lonely kid, and books allowed me to escape."

"How old were you when you were making your own dinner?"

"Eight. Before that I would make sandwiches or eat cheese and crackers or whatever else I found in the fridge."

"That's awful young to be left alone," said Raven.

"I didn't know any better, and I did have my dad's brother I could call if anything got too bad. Though I never called, because I knew it would lead to a fight."

"What happened to Turtle?"

He took a deep breath. "My mom and I killed her."

She stared at him a moment, not sure she'd heard him correctly. 'How?"

"Dad was supposed to come home one day, but the weather delayed his flight. My mother was in a play, and several of the cast were at our place for the evening, running lines." He shifted in his seat and looked up at her. "I was happy when she had the cast over because I often got treats. Like salami or strawberries or, like that evening, grapes. I sat up in my room reading a book to Turtle, eating grapes and sharing them with her. I didn't know cats shouldn't eat grapes."

He stopped and took a deep breath as though gathering the courage to tell her more, though she could imagine what came next. She had seen cats like that come in to the vet practice a few times. Some made it. Some didn't.

"When Turtle got sick, I ran to tell Mom, and she told me to go back to my room and go to sleep. She said the cat would be fine. I don't imagine she knew cats shouldn't eat grapes either. This was before the internet. At around midnight, I finally fell asleep holding poor Turtle, but the next day she still wasn't well. When Dad got home, I ran to tell him right away. He dropped his bag in the front hall, took the cat to the vet, and came back three hours later to tell me Turtle was gone."

"Oh, Lance, that must have been so hard." She reached out and placed her hand on his arm, feeling so much for the boy he once was. "You were only nine."

"Well, that was just the beginning." He swallowed hard. "When Dad came home, he and Mom got into a major fight. Worse than any I'd witnessed before. She was crying and saying she hadn't meant for the cat to die. He was yelling that he couldn't trust her, and what if it were me next time? I went to my room and hid in the closet, holding my hands over my ears. I'd never felt so alone in my life."

"So what happened?" Raven found herself asking.

"Well, when the fight was over, Dad came into my room and said we had to go."

"You mean he kicked you and your mother out?"

"No." He shook his head. "He helped me pack up my stuff, and he and I want to stay with my Uncle Gil."

"Wow, that must have been hard."

"Yes, and of course I blamed myself, because if I hadn't killed Turtle, it wouldn't have happened. As it was, I didn't see my mother again for years, until I went to a show she was in."

"You never saw your mother? Why not?"

"You sure you want to hear all this?"

"Of course," said Raven. She believed sharing things like this helped take away their power, and he needed to tell someone.

"Well, about a year after we left, I was living with my Uncle Gil, and I finally got up the courage to ask him why my mother never visited. It was around Mother's Day, and we were supposed to make presents for our mothers at school."

"Gil was really quiet and said he had to talk to my father. I heard one side of that call, even though Gil hadn't meant for me to hear. I don't think houses had good insulation back then." He laughed softly.

She squeezed his arm and stayed silent, waiting for him to continue.

"Gil was mad at my father, told him I had a right to know where my mother was. I take it Dad gave him permission to tell me."

"Turns out that the woman I knew as Mom was my stepmother. My birth mother had died from some kind of cancer when I was two. Dad had married my step-mother six months later."

"Oh, Lance, that's so much loss for a little kid." Raven just wanted to hug him.

"If Dad had come home on schedule, Turtle might have lived, but their marriage was destined to break down eventually. Still, I blamed myself for years." He shook himself, as though coming back to the present. "So that's why I don't want to get close to cats. I killed my cat, and my parents' marriage ended, and my life changed. All in one horrible night."

They sat like that together for a few minutes while she digested what he'd told her. No wonder he wanted to control things where he could. "Your uncle sounds nice."

"Gil was a great guy. A lot like Betty is. Like my father was. I got lucky being born into this family."

"Did you live with him long?"

"Uncle Gil is the reason I went into plumbing. I began to help him on the worksite on weekends when I was fourteen or so. I graduated from high school, got my apprenticeship. Then when he died, I took over the business and helped my aunt raise my younger cousins."

"How old were you when that happened?"

"Twenty."

"Twenty? You took over a business when you were twenty?"

"Yes. I was lucky Gil had loyal employees who stuck with me for years. And my aunt managed a lot of the scheduling, just as she had when he was alive. They kind of plugged me into the business where Gil had been, and I learned fast. I basically asked myself every day, What would Uncle Gil do?"

He pointed to the tattoo on his forearm: and anchor with a wheel. "I even got the same tattoo." He laughed. "To remind myself that I needed to be the anchor of the family and keep everyone moving forward together."

"A lot of responsibility for a young man."

He shrugged. "No more than a lot of single moms take on. At least I had a lot of people to rely on." He smiled. "And a few to give me a kick up the backside when I needed it."

CHAPTER 14

*L*ance had been sitting too long, and a crick in his neck begged to be stretched, but he endured it a little longer so that Raven would stay there with her hand on his arm. But eventually it grew more painful, and he had to move.

He sat back in the chair, and disappointment descended when her hand slipped to her lap. He couldn't remember the last time anyone had touched him for that long. Even before his marriage ended, it had been devoid of physical intimacy.

"Sorry to burden you with all that. It hit me when I saw that cat."

"Don't worry about it." She flushed as though embarrassed for him—or maybe she felt the sudden loss of touch too?

He knew little about her. Certainly not as much as she knew about him. His gaze left her face and wandered to the window. "The curtains fit perfectly," he said. "Thank you again for making them. You are a woman of many talents."

"I wouldn't go that far," she said. "These were my first try at sewing, and I had help."

"Your first try?"

"I took a class and learned how," she said. "The local fabric shop offers a kind of tutoring to help people with projects they're working on."

"You found a class and made curtains in the past week? What are you, some kind of saint?"

"No, I just felt so bad, and then when I found out you were my new partner in this venture, I wanted to show you that you could rely on me."

"You didn't need to go that far," he said, but when her face fell, he remembered Betty's comment about him being intimidating to others. "Though I am pleased you did," he added. "They're perfect." He didn't add that whenever he saw them, he would think of her and her kindness. He might tell her one day, once he knew her better.

She was the first woman he had met in months whom he wished to know better.

"We should probably go back in if you're ready," she said.

"Yes, the rain seems to have stopped, and Zoey and Axel will be wondering where we went. Did she notice me leaving?"

"No. they were too busy with the cats and their conversation. Have they been together long?"

"I don't know, though it seems obvious that her friend is more than a friend."

She laughed. "No doubt about it at all. That man is smitten with your daughter."

"Did you say *smitten*? I haven't heard that word in years."

"My mother used to say it," said Raven.

"Were you close to your mother?"

"Oh, yes. We were close. Until we weren't."

"That sounds like a story worth hearing."

"I suppose, but it will have to wait. We have a venture to plan, and your consultants await."

She moved to stand, and he leaned across the table and grabbed her hand so she would turn back to look at him. "Thanks for listening,"

"Don't worry about it," she said, looking at his hand and then into his eyes. Her tongue darted out to wet her lips, and he wondered if she would let him kiss her right now. He decided not to try. What if she slapped him?

Instead, he said, "If you ever need someone to listen, you know where to find me."

"Yes," she whispered, swallowing hard. She seemed attracted to him, too. Good to know.

He slowly sat back and let go of her hand. She didn't snatch it back as though burned. Instead, she stayed a beat or two longer, her eyes searching his.

Yes, there was definitely some kind of chemistry happening here, and he wished to explore it further. He should at least try.

He would try.

He leaned toward her, and she didn't move, only licked her lips again. He put his palms on the table, leaned in further, and noticed her move a little closer too. The scent of a familiar flower wafted toward him, and he breathed it in, trying to place the scent as they drew closer, her eyes drifting closed in anticipation.

And then there was the crunch of footsteps on the gravel outside.

He pulled back just as the door opened, and Raven grimaced as though she was just as displeased. They would have to table this until another time.

"Dad, what are you doing in here? Axel got the webcam figured out. All he needs now is the laptop."

"We were just on our way back," he said. "We thought we would wait for the rain to stop first." Out of Zoey's line of sight, he winked at Raven, and she gave him a quick conspiratorial grin before sliding out of the booth seat and climbing out of the camper.

Lance waited a moment before he followed, and when he did, the air felt different. It could have been that the rain had washed away all the haze and left things fresh, but he knew better. He had just forgiven himself and unloaded a burden he had carried for years.

He walked back into where Axel was conferring with Raven about where best to place the webcam, and he walked over to Tilly's cage. The little cat was awake now, and she walked right up to him as though she knew him. Silently he thanked the little cat for unlocking all that pent-up anguish he had carried for so long.

"Well, little one," he said. "Let's find you a new forever home, shall we?"

Tilly butted her head up against his hand for a pet and purred in agreement.

CHAPTER 15

*O*nce they'd talked through where best to mount the webcam, Raven told Axel and Zoey where to find the tools and ladder. Then she slipped into the kitchen while Lance was petting Tilly. *Coward*, she berated herself when she got to the kitchen, leaning against the other side of the closed door. She couldn't face him on her own again so soon.

What had she been thinking? Lance—her new *business* partner—had been about to kiss her, and she didn't stop him.

Oh no. Far from it. She'd been a willing accomplice. She'd leaned closer, willing him to kiss her. Willing him to put into practice what she had been thinking about for days.

He was to be avoided. After all, he hated cats, and cats were her life's work.

Though, she reminded herself, that little objection was no longer valid. He didn't hate cats, nor was he allergic to them. In fact, he loved cats so much that losing one had scarred him for life.

She needed to stop thinking like this and do something, so she walked to the fridge, took out the large pot of soup she'd made, and placed it on the stove to warm up. Then she pulled out the ingredients for sandwiches, brewed a pot of coffee and put the cookies she'd promised into the oven.

Satisfied, she had given Zoey and Axel enough time to retrieve the tools, she opened the door to find Lance on the ladder, screwing the camera into the wall while Axel and Zoey directed the placement.

"What do you think?" asked Axel, when she stepped into the room. "You can turn it with this remote control, and you can point it into all three back pens. And it zooms in. See?" Axel turned the computer toward her and showed her on the webcam app he had downloaded. "This link here," he said, pointing to the code on the bottom of the page, "can be pasted onto the website. I can do it if you give me admin access."

Raven avoided the smoldering look Lance sent in her direction as he dismounted the ladder, and focused on what Axel was showing her. "That would be perfect. If you're sure it won't take much time."

"Half an hour at most, I would think."

"Well, first let's have lunch. I've got a pot of soup simmering on the stove, and sandwiches."

"Sounds great," said Axel. "I am a little hungry."

"You are always hungry," said Zoey.

"Come, then." Raven led the three into the house and showed them where the restroom was so they could wash up.

Zoey returned first. "Can I help?"

"Sure. You can set the table. Cutlery is in that drawer, and napkins are in the one below. Just spoons."

Zoey set the table and returned to the island, where Raven was standing near the stove. "Are you and my dad dating?"

The spoon she was stirring with slipped from her hands, and she rushed to grab it. "No. We only met a few days ago."

"But you like him?"

"He seems like a nice man," said Raven, careful to keep her voice neutral. She wanted to tell Zoey to mind her own business, but that would only raise more questions.

"Mom divorced him over six months ago, but they've been separated for close to two years. You know, if you're worried it's too soon."

"Zoey, where is this coming from?" She looked at Zoey from the corner of her eye and kept stirring the soup.

Zoey bent her head and whispered, "I just don't want him to be alone."

"You should talk to him about it. Maybe he's already seeing someone. I'm sure an attractive man like him won't be alone long if he wants a relationship."

"So, you think he's attractive?" Zoey looked up, a spark of hope in her eyes.

But Raven didn't have to answer that question, because Lance and Axel walked back into the kitchen. "Zoey, check out this eagle out the back window," said Axel.

He led her down the small hallway and to the large window where Raven knew you could see a pair of eagles nesting about a hundred yards from the house.

"What can I do to help?" Lance placed his hands on the island between them, close enough that she could smell the soap he used.

You could help by finishing that kiss you started was the thought that popped into her head, but she shoved it away. "You could tell me what kind of sandwiches you all like."

A buzzer went off, reminding her to take the cookies out of the oven.

"You get that, and I'll start with the sandwiches," he said, walking around the counter and taking the butter knife she was holding from her hand. Oh my. He was so close she could feel the heat emanating from his chest.

"Sure." She let go of the knife and backed away, grabbing a pair of oven mitts and removing the baking sheet from the oven.

When she turned, he'd already buttered eight pieces of bread and added lettuce to one side of each. "Turkey or beef?" he asked her.

"Turkey, please."

"Condiments?"

"Just some mayo, cheddar cheese, salt and pepper, and a slice of tomato."

"Sounds good."

He made three that way and asked Axel what he preferred. In a matter of a few minutes, four sliced sandwiches and four bowls of soup sat on the table.

Raven followed with glasses and a pitcher of water, and they soon were enjoying the meal together while talking about websites and cats.

Two hours later, with Axel's skill at asking the right questions, they had decided on the referral process, added all the forms and webcam links to both websites, and put in an order through an online printing company for cards with the QR code on the back.

"This looks fantastic," said Lance, as Axel walked them through what he had done and how to do any updates they required.

"Glad you like it," said Axel. "And I'll put together that template we talked about. The one that you can use to introduce each of the cats. It will help increase interest if people have an introduction to them and can watch them on the website.

"Thank you, Axel. I love that idea, and I am sure Mal will be into helping with that. She loves to write."

"This is a great initiative. I'm glad I could help."

"We'll add the same-day service to your bill, Dad," Zoey joked.

"Zoey, stop. I'm happy to help," said Axel. "Though I would still love to go on a fishing trip."

"Let me know when you're available. I can go on a Sunday night if I'm back Monday evening or early Tuesday morning to open the store. We could go up to Campbell River. There's a lot of great fishing up that way. "

"I would love to see more of the island," said Axel. "All right, Zo?"

"Absolutely," said Zoey. "Maybe Raven could come too."

"Perhaps," said Raven, who grew warm when Lance turned to her and smiled.

When they left, she would have to find the old tent she kept in the garage and make sure rodents or mold hadn't got to it.

Just in case.

CHAPTER 16

*L*ance was tired as he drove them into town. Though all he really wanted to do was sleep, it was only four o'clock when they pulled into town. The rain clouds had moved over to the mainland, leaving behind blue skies and sunshine.

"What do you two want to do this afternoon?" he asked.

"I noticed a club for dancing," said Zoey. "Thought we might go there tonight."

"You two can go without me," said Lance. Even a thirtysomething would feel old in the place she was referring to. "I have some work to do at the store."

What he had was a book he wanted to read, but they didn't need to know that. "Thought we could head out to Parksville for dinner then take a walk on the beach. I can have you back by eight. The club doesn't get busy until nine."

"Perfect," said Axel.

They drove out to the seafood restaurant Lance had heard was good. Over dinner, Axel told him about growing up in Alberta, playing hockey on a backyard ice rink, and living in a small town not unlike Sunshine Bay.

"I miss the community aspects," said Axel. "Which I suppose is why I enjoy working with nonprofits so much. But I don't miss everyone knowing everything about you. My parents want me to move back, but I'm not sure I'd be happy there now that I've lived near the ocean."

"It is beautiful out here. I suppose that is why they call it 'Beautiful British Columbia.'"

They left the restaurant and headed toward the beach, where Lance bought them ice cream. Axel walked down by the shore to watch the creatures in a tide pool, and Zoey stayed up on the boardwalk with Lance.

"He may have to go back to Alberta one day," said

Zoey. "It's just too expensive to live in Vancouver. At least if you ever want to own a home."

"Yes, Toronto is expensive too," said Lance. "That was one reason I opted for a small town, where I can own a building rather than just a condo."

"You own the building where the store is?" asked Zoey. "The hardware store, too?"

"Yes. My uncle once had part ownership in that store," said Lance. "Now I rent the space, along with the two apartments above and the chocolate shop next door. The entire street has apartments above the stores. Except mine. Mine is the only one with the apartment on both levels, because of Betty."

"So, you did okay in the divorce," said Zoey.

"Your mother and I owned two properties other than our house, so yes."

"Oh, good. I've been worried about you, Dad."

"There's no reason to worry about me. I'm fine."

"But I thought, now that Mom…" She peered up into his eyes. "Did Chelsea or Mom talk to you in the past few days?"

"No. I haven't spoken to your mother since we signed the papers."

"That's why," she whispered.

"That's why what?" He turned to her, concerned. "What's wrong?"

"Mom should be the one to tell you, but I know Chelsea is upset about it, so…" She took a deep breath as though deciding whether to be the one to break the news.

"I was wondering why you hadn't said anything. Mom's engaged, and Chelsea is really upset. Mom phoned me to ask if I had heard from her, because I guess Chelsea just left the house when Mom announced it to her."

"Why didn't you say something?"

"Because I called Chelsea. She's staying with a friend. I guess she needs time to think. And she told me not to tell you, or you would worry. I thought Mom would tell you, but I guess she didn't want to worry you either."

He took his phone out of his pocket and dialed Chelsea's number. It rang half a dozen times and then went to voice mail. He left a message for her to call him, then dialed Marlene's number, though it was almost ten at night there.

"Hello, Lance," she said, and he could hear in her voice that she did not want to talk to him.

"I haven't been able to reach Chelsea, and I wondered if everything is okay."

"Oh, yes. She's staying with a friend for the weekend. That's all."

"You spoke to her in the last couple of days, then?" he pressed.

She sighed, and he could hear tears in her voice. "No. Lance, I don't know where she is. We had a fight, and she packed a bag and left the house. Said she would stay with a friend. I trust that's what she's doing."

"I see," he said. "What did you fight about?"

Zoey walked down the boardwalk to give him privacy and to catch up with Axel.

"We fought about you," she said.

"Me?"

"Lance, I am getting married again, and Chelsea was

upset about it. She blamed you for our divorce—but now, it appears, she blames me."

"Why would she blame either of us? We agreed to part on good terms, to not talk about it to our kids, didn't we?"

"You know how kids are. They often need someone to blame."

"I thought you were going to talk to her about it. Make her see that this is a mutual decision."

"I did, but she thought you didn't do enough to hold our family together. That as soon as you could, you left her, the business, everything."

"But you corrected her misperceptions, right?"

"I tried, but she had a point. You did just leave town."

"I left *town*. I didn't leave *her*."

"I know. But she didn't see it that way, especially since Zoey left too. It's been a lot of change."

"What kind of guy are you marrying? Is he nice to her?"

She sighed. "I'm marrying Brad."

"Brad? My friend Brad?"

"Yes. We've been seeing each other for a while, and it just kind of happened."

"How long?" he asked, feeling dizzy.

She didn't answer.

He walked down the boardwalk to a bench and sat down, thinking back to when he'd last spoken to Brad. Not since he'd left Toronto, and even before that they had been drifting apart. In fact, they hadn't seen much of each other since he and Marlene had entered mediation.

"Were you seeing him before we separated, Marlene? Before we started mediation?"

"No," she breathed. "But we started seeing each other just after you and I called it quits."

"So, throughout the last mediation talks, when I was pouring out my heart, blaming myself for not being good enough, for not listening enough, you were manipulating me? All after you had already found your next husband?"

"No. That's not true. Everything we talked about,

everything that wasn't working between us, that was real."

"But you failed to tell me everything, didn't you? I know we had our differences, but I never betrayed you. Ever." He wished he had a punching bag nearby, or at least a pillow.

"I'm sorry, Lance. It just happened, and it wasn't until after we separated."

"You should have said something. You should have told me you had already moved on with my former friend. I did nothing to deserve this."

"We had already ended things, Lance. I didn't betray you."

"If I had done that to you with one of your friends, tell me you wouldn't feel betrayed," he spat into the phone.

She gasped as though he had doused her in ice water. "I didn't think about it that way."

"And on top of that, when Chelsea blamed me, you didn't do your best to stop that. I never believed this of you, Marlene. I thought the deal we came up with was something I could honor, and I trusted you to do the same."

"I'm sorry. I didn't mean for this to happen. It hasn't been easy since you left."

"It hasn't been easy for me either," he said. "I gave up my whole life so you could be free to be with my friend. When Chelsea calls or comes home, tell her I want to speak with her. I'm worried about her."

Silence.

"Marlene, promise me you'll tell Chelsea I want to talk to her."

"Okay," she said. "I promise. And for what it's worth, I'm sorry."

He hung up and sat on the bench, staring out at sea and feeling like an idiot. All that time he had been doing the work to save their marriage, and she was already seeing Brad. Why hadn't she said something?

But he knew why. It was because she wanted Lance to finish the house so they could sell it and make a profit. All that time he had spent alone, working through his anger and pain, blaming himself as he tore out walls and rebuilt them until the house was unrecognizable, had been so they could make a few more bucks.

He glanced down the beach at Zoey and Axel and told himself to get it together. They didn't need to be involved in his divorce drama and, unlike Marlene, he would not speak ill of her to either of his daughters. He walked away from them down the beach, staring out at sea until he had calmed down. He took a quick snap at the setting sun, then turned back toward them.

"Well," he said when they were within earshot, "we should get you back to town if you're going to go dancing tonight."

Zoey searched his face but just returned his smile. "Looking forward to it. I hope they have a good band."

The drive back was quiet except for the eighties rock music coming from the radio, and when they arrived, he saw that both Axel and Zoey had drifted off to sleep.

He smiled, pleased that at least one of his daughters was doing well.

Marlene was probably right that Chelsea would eventually be okay too, but he still wanted to see her. If he didn't hear from her in the next day or so, he would ask Betty to watch the store for a few days while he went out east.

The following morning, he dropped off Zoey and Axel at the ferry.

"Thanks for everything," he said. "I love the changes you made to the website."

"No problem, sir… Lance," Axel said. "I look forward to seeing the cats here next time we visit."

"I'll set up that fishing trip soon," he promised, "and I'll let Zoey know a few weeks ahead so you can plan."

"Thanks, Dad." Zoey hugged him tight. "I'll tell you when I hear from Chelsea."

He returned her hug and felt a little catch in his throat as he waved them off.

It was always hard to say goodbye.

CHAPTER 17

*O*n Tuesday afternoon, Raven put on a new dress because, she told herself, it felt like an occasion. Around the necks of two cats, she fastened collars with heart-shaped tags that read *Adopt me*. One was Tilly, and the other was a gray named Sea Smoke who had to be rehoused when his owner went into care. She drove the cats into town.

When she arrived, the store was full of children and their parents, many of them purchasing the latest book Pinky had been reading. Ahmed met her at the door and quickly took Tilly's carrier from her. "We should probably go straight back if we don't want to attract too much attention. Let the cats settle first."

She smiled gratefully started to slip down a back aisle when Pinky chose that moment to look up from the cash register. "Oh, how exciting! You're here!"

Heads swiveled to face her, and a little boy demanded, "Is that the new cat?" Several children rushed toward Raven, and for a moment she knew exactly how a rock star must feel when mobbed by fans. They weren't tall enough to pull out her hair, and they probably wouldn't try to rip off pieces her skirt, but she still froze and scanned the room to determine her best exit strategy.

"Stop!" A girl of about six ran toward her and faced the growing number of children rushing in her direction. The tiny mob stopped in its tracks. "Cats don't like crowds," the girl said. "We must take turns and look one at a time."

She turned to Raven and pointed to a chair at the end of the nearby aisle. "Set her down there on that chair." Raven did as she was told and watched as, remarkably, the children formed a line and calmly stepped forward, one by one, to look at the cat.

"What's his name?" said one little boy.

"Looks like a Shadow," said another.

"Or Duster," said a third.

"I want to pet him!" said another.

"No," said the girl, pushing the boy's hand away from the cage. "You can't just pet him. He doesn't like that. Cats need to ask to be petted."

Raven stood aside, allowing the child to take charge. She had the makings of a prime minister. Under her guidance, the children each looked at the cat then returned to their parents. Only a few needed to be promised that they could of course come back soon.

"Thank you for your help," said Raven to the girl, after the rest of the children were gone. "You know a lot about cats."

"I know this cat," she said, stooping down to the cat's level.

"Abby, this isn't Sea Smoke. Grandma had to give him up, remember?"

Her father grabbed her hand and tried to pull her away, but she slipped out of his grasp and returned to talk to the cat.

"I'm sorry," he said to Raven. "My grandmother had to go into a home recently, and we were away when it happened. I had promised Abby she could have Sea

Smoke—my grandmother's cat—if he ever needed a home. But we were away two months, and my mother must have forgotten. Or maybe she didn't think I was serious."

"Well, I've had this cat for two months out at my farm. I was told his name is, indeed, Sea Smoke, and that he was given up by his owner when she went into care."

The cat stepped toward Abby and butted her little fingers with his head.

"See, Daddy?" Abby said, looking up at her father. "He's asking me to pet him just like he used to do at Grandma's house. It *is* Sea Smoke."

Her father looked at the cat, and his daughter, and then up at Raven. "I think she's right. It does appear to be the same cat. Is there any way of finding out exactly who gave him up?"

"Just a moment," said Raven, bringing out her phone. "I'll check my email. I'm pretty sure the vet told me." She scrolled through the emails from Rosalyn and found the one she was looking for. Yes, a Beryl Butter—"

"Butterfield," said Abby. "That is our last name. I am Abigail Butterfield."

"It appears you are correct. This is Sea Smoke Butterfield."

"Can we take him home?" asked Abby.

"What do you need for us to adopt him?" asked her father.

"Well, I wasn't expecting this to happen quite so quickly, but we have application forms on the counter to fill out."

"Lead on," said Mr. Butterfield.

Raven took him to the counter and handed him a pen and the application form. When he'd completed it, she looked it over, asked him a few quick questions, and told him about the suggested donation she normally collected to cover the costs of care.

"When would you like to pick him up?" asked Raven.

"Can't we take him now, Daddy?"

"Yes, of course." He turned to her and took out his credit card. "Where can I make the donation?"

"Pinky can help us with that," said Raven.

They paid the fee, and Raven carried the cat to their car.

"You can use the carrier. Just bring it back to the store in the next couple of days, please." She set the cat into the back seat and waved them off, her heart soaring at how happy the little girl had been.

She returned to the store to find Ahmed. She had brought Sea Smoke as an alternate first pick just in case Lance had reservations about having Turtle's doppelgänger living here. Now she was eager to see how Tilly was getting along.

When she arrived, Pinky was relating the tale of Sea Smoke to Ahmed and Lance, the latter of whom had Tilly curled up against his chest.

"Can you believe this? We haven't even officially kicked off, and already we have a successful outcome," said Raven.

"And several customers bent on returning next week, I hear," said Lance, as he stroked the cat's fur. "I imagine this one will find a home soon too. Meanwhile, let's move her into her pen so we can introduce her to Rhett."

Lance wedged the door open and shook a box of Rhett's favorite treats. A few moments later, the familiar black-and-white cat appeared, took the treat from Lance's outstretched hand, ate it with quiet dignity—as befitting his gentlemanly status—then walked past Tilly's pen, tail high in the air, and back to the store to find his favorite shelf.

"So far, so good," said Raven.

"I suppose we'll know more once she is out and about in the store," said Lance. "Do you want to put her in the window today? It's not too warm for her there yet. And if we leave Curtis's trap door open, she can leave if it gets too uncomfortable."

"Maybe for an hour or so," she said. "Tilly has a bit of a fear of loud noises. I think she endured a thunderstorm a few nights before they found her."

"No time like the present," said Lance, picking up Tilly and taking her to the window. Raven pulled out an information sheet about Tilly, happy she had the foresight to put together one for each cat, and placed it into the plastic sleeve Curtis had put into the window. Now people would know about her. It gave her name, gender, age, and breed. At the bottom she'd listed the website, along with the QR code Axel had generated for them.

"Nice touch," said Lance, and Raven beamed at him, pleased that he was pleased.

Their gazes met, and she immediately busied herself by rummaging in her tote bag. "I brought some flyers and brochures as well. The printer was quick to get them to me. I only ordered them on Saturday." She pulled a few from her bag and handed them over.

"They turned out well," he said. "You'd think we spent a lot more than an afternoon planning these out."

"Zoey is a wiz with graphic design," said Raven. "And Axel pulled it all together on the website in a way that is easy to navigate and understand. I may get his number from you and ask him to redesign the rest of my site for me. Once several more of the rescues are adopted, I'll have more kennel space available."

"I'll ask Zoey for his email address," said Lance. "I'm sure he would be delighted. He really enjoys working with community groups."

"Does Zoey freelance too? I'll need a new logo for the nonprofit arm once I get it approved."

"I am sure she'd be happy to help. I've been told that she and a lot of her friends have what they call side hustles."

"It's good experience. I've always had at least two income streams," said Raven.

"I know about the cats. What else?"

"Rental income, and I have a few regular tax customers. Keeps my hand in the world of accounting, which reminds me... I was wondering if you have time for coffee. I'm meeting my vet friend Rosalyn at the Whisk to talk about the nonprofit paperwork, and I thought you might like to meet her. If anything happens with the cats, she has assured me you can call her directly, but it might be good to put a face to a name."

"Sure, let me just tell Ahmed. I can only go until three. He has an appointment, and having only one person here, especially when we have a new cat, seems risky."

Raven nodded in agreement, remembering the small stampede that Sea Smoke had brought on. "That would be perfect. You wouldn't want to sit through our paperwork discussions, anyway."

Ten minutes later, Raven was introducing Lance to Rosalyn over a cup of coffee and sharing the news about their first adoption.

"Fantastic news," said Rosalyn. "Let's hope it's a good omen." She handed Lance her business card. "My practice is close by," she said. "Just turn right at the intersection near your store and head away from the ocean. It's an old wartime house that we renovated."

Lance drank his coffee and listened patiently as Rosalyn told him all about the information and services she could provide to customers who adopted.

"Oh, and before I forget, here's a stack of coupon cards." She handed them to Raven. "Anyone who adopts a cat through this program gets a ten-percent discount off their first treatment. Of course, I examine them and make sure they have their shots before they even go to your store."

"That's generous of you," said Lance.

Rosalyn shrugged. "Rave and I have been helping cats find homes for years. It's our pet project." She laughed at the pun, and Raven rolled her eyes. "It's also one way to make sure the new placement is working out and an opportunity to give advice or information the new owners may need."

"Ah, so there is an ulterior motive," Lance said. He smiled at Raven a beat too long, and she returned the smile until they were interrupted by a *beep beep beep*.

"That's my reminder," Lance said, turning the alarm off on his watch. "I have to get back to the store. I promised Ahmed I would be on time, as it's his wedding anniversary today. Thirty-eight years."

"Best not be late, then," said Rosalyn.

"Do you want to bring another cat by in the next day or so?" he asked Raven. "I feel like we've had some great luck so far."

"I'll stop by tomorrow afternoon," said Raven. "But if anything happens with Tilly before that, call me, and we can figure out a solution, okay?"

He said his goodbyes and shook Rosalyn's hand again. "Nice to know you're on board," he said. And then he walked out of the bistro.

"Yummy," said Rosalyn as she watched him leave. "What's the story? Is he married?"

"Divorced," said Raven, "and, according to his daughter, he's available, and it isn't too soon for him to start a new relationship."

"What?" Rosalyn laughed, and Raven told her about the conversation she had with Zoey, about the work she and her boyfriend had done on the site, and the almost kiss.

"He almost kissed you?"

"Yes."

"Were you disappointed he didn't?"

Raven felt herself flush, and Rosalyn laughed. "You were! That's huge, Rave. When was the last time you kissed a man? A few years ago? That lumberjack guy who worked on the first stages of the shelter?"

"Let's just say it's been a while—not that it's any of your concern," Raven said sternly, eliciting more laughter from her friend.

"Well, I approve of this one," said Rosalyn. "You even have his daughter's approval."

"Early days," said Raven. "We didn't hit it off right away, and he has a tendency to want to take over. You know how I feel about that."

"You only approve of six-year-old girls taking charge?"

"That kid was intimidating."

"A little like you when you're in full Raven mode."

"Really?"

"You can be intimidating, Rave. And you do tend to push people away. Especially men."

"Still, I don't want to ever get into another relationship like I had with Duane."

"This guy's not a Duane. Duane was more self-centered and entitled. Lance looks more like a tradesperson, like he could earn his living with his hands if he needed to."

"Actually, he used to be a plumber."

"See? A guy who enjoys helping others solve problems, whereas Duane loved to create problems for other people to solve."

"Starting with me," said Raven.

"Exactly," said Rosalyn. "You could do worse than Lance."

"And, as you have so handily pointed out, I did do worse. Much worse."

They broke into laughter, and then Rosalyn leaned toward her. "Seriously, I would love to see you find someone to love again. If his daughter who thinks highly of him, approves of you, and he has muscles like that one, all the better."

"Maybe you're right. He's certainly growing on me." And he was invading her thoughts a few dozen times a day. But Rosalyn didn't need to know that, so she changed the subject to Rosalyn's daughter. As she listened to the detailed description only a devoted mother could provide, she smiled to herself and allowed her mind to drift again to the man down the street.

Maybe Rosalyn was right, and it was time to see if a new man could fit into her life. For the first time in years, she wanted to find out.

CHAPTER 18

When Lance walked back to the store with a takeaway dinner from the local Greek restaurant, he was surprised that Rhett Butler wasn't in his usual spot in front of the apartment door. "Rhett?" he called.

Mrwow. He turned to find the cat sitting in front of the door that led to the cat pens.

"There you are. Are you coming?" Lance unlocked the apartment and pushed open the door. Rhett didn't move from his spot. *Mroww!*

"You can stay here if you want to." Lance stepped inside and closed the door, placing his meal on the kitchen counter.

Mroww! Even behind the closed door, he could hear the cat.

"Okay, I'm coming," He went back to the door and opened it to find Rhett still sitting outside the door to the pens. Rhett was clearly trying to tell him something.

Mroeww, mrooww. Rhett walked over to Lance, rubbed against his leg, then returned to his spot in front of the closed door.

Lance walked closer and could now hear Tilly answering Rhett's calls.

"You want to go inside?" he asked the cat. He opened the door and Rhett ran inside to Tilly's pen. *Mrewww, mroww.*

They touched noses through the spaces in the wire mesh.

"Okay, I get it," said Lance, opening the pen to let Rhett inside. But instead, Tilly slipped out and followed Rhett out the door and down the hall. Lance turned to follow and found the pair sitting in front of the apartment door.

"Seriously?" Lance got to the door and looked down on the pair. Rhett looked up at him.

Mrewow.

"Well, she's your guest. You're going to have to show her around."

Mreoww.

"Fine." He opened the door, and the pair went inside and leaped onto the couch. Lance put his meal onto a plate, put it into the microwave, and put an extra bowl of dry cat food beside Rhett's bowl. Then he walked to the living room, put his food onto a tray table, and turned on the television. When a commercial came on, he glanced over and found the pair sleeping side by side.

"Well, Rhett, it looks like your guest likes it here." The older cat opened his eyes, looked at Lance, closed them again, snuggled closer to Tilly, and purred.

"Thanks, buddy. Now I just feel like a third wheel."

It was time to do something about that.

Lance woke on Wednesday, restless and worried that he had yet to hear from Chelsea. Before he booked his flights and connected with his aunt to see if she could come back to watch over the store for a week, he dialed Marlene's house number to ask for updates.

"Hello?"

"Chelsea?" He tamped down the rising anger. Why had neither she nor her mother seen fit to call him and put him out of his misery? He hadn't slept well in two days. "Are you okay?"

"Who is it?" he heard Marlene ask. "Whoever it is, take a message. We need to talk about this, and you aren't going out. Not after what you put me through."

"It's *my dad*," Chelsea hissed, and he pulled the phone away from his ear, even though he knew his youngest child's anger and contempt were directed toward Marlene and not, for the first time in months, at him. It was rather a relief.

"Tell him I want to talk to him."

"Tell him yourself," she said. He heard footsteps, and Chelsea finally said, "Sorry, Dad. I just had to find a place to sit"—a door slammed— "where *I can get some privacy.*" She was yelling now. "Sorry," she said into the phone. "Didn't mean to shout at you."

"Things sound a little tense there," he said. "Are you okay?"

There was no response, and then he heard sobbing. "Oh, Daddy, I am so sorry," she wailed.

Daddy? She never called him that. He wished he could somehow beam himself to Toronto to hug her, to reassure her that things couldn't be as bad as she thought. He hated feeling helpless. "What are you sorry about?"

"I blamed you for the divorce. But I didn't know it was all Mom's fault."

"Chelsea, your mother and I explained this when I left. It's no one's fault. We just want different things now."

"How can you say that, Dad? She's with Uncle Brad. And they've been together for like years."

He listened to her cry for a few minutes, trying to think of something to say that might help. Maybe an analogy? "Chelsea, you know how you're interested in going to university next year?"

"Yeah." She sniffled a bit. "I am going, Dad. I'll get a loan if I have to."

"Of course you are, and we told you we would help you with your tuition and rent. You still have our support. That's not why I brought it up." Even when he was trying to help, he got things wrong.

"Why did you bring it up?"

"Well, I guess to draw a comparison, for discussion purposes."

"Is this one of your lectures?"

"No. I just have a couple of questions for you to think about. It might help you understand why your mother and I aren't together anymore."

She sniffled. "Okay, ask your questions."

"Okay, so your friends, are all of them going to go into pre-med?"

"No, of course not."

"And is that their fault?"

"No. We're all just different."

"Even your friends that you've done a lot of things with, like playing in the school band together, playing volleyball together?"

"None of them want to be a doctor. Half of them think they're going to be internet influencers and just talk about clothes all day."

He smiled and shook his head. At least her contempt wasn't reserved for her parents alone. "And when you go off to university, you'll probably find other people you like. New people who are also interested in medical school."

"That's the plan," she said. "Where are you going with this?"

"Well, your mother and I worked together a long time, just like you have gone to school with your friends for a long time. She helped me when I took over my uncle's business, and I supported her when she wanted to be an X-ray technician. When we updated all those houses, we worked hard, and together we raised you and your sister. But now we're interested in different things, like you're interested in different things than your high school friends are."

"But you were married. You were supposed to stay together for life."

"I used to think that too," said Lance. "I certainly tried to. But your mother and I want very different things. She wants to continue to update houses and build her career in real estate, and I just want to live a quiet rural life, read books, and go fishing. Can you imagine your mother being happy going fishing every weekend?"

"Dad, there's more to life than fishing. You could have stayed and made it work."

"I did stay. For years. And so did your mom, but we just don't want the same things. I didn't want to fix houses anymore, Chelsea. I was sick of being a plumber, and I don't like the big networking parties she thrives on. All I want is a nice place in the country."

"So you didn't leave because of her and Uncle Brad?"

"No. Your mother and I spent months in mediation talking through what we wanted and what we didn't want. We talked about the compromises we would have to make. We decided that the thing we both loved most was you and Zoey. And that won't change. But we really had grown in different directions. We just want different things now."

"But why did you have to leave me?" Her tears were back.

"I didn't leave you. I'm still here when you need me. Just a call away. And any time you want, I can send you a ticket to visit."

"You could have stayed."

"Yes, you're right. And maybe I should have stayed. But living alone in that big house, while you were living in the apartment with your mom? It was hard."

"Did you move because I didn't visit?"

"No. I moved because I got an offer on the business, and I really wanted to buy the Bookworm."

"So, Mom was right?"

"That no one was to blame?"

"Yeah." She sighed.

"Yes, I suppose in this case, your mother is correct." He laughed, knowing that the girls thought their mother was right most of the time.

"I'm sorry I've been so mean to you, Dad."

"You were hurting. And it's been a big adjustment for all of us."

"That's what Zoey said. She said you even adjusted so much you have a cat." Chelsea laughed. "And that it bosses you around."

"Yes, Rhett Butler came with the store. And right now, I have another cat living here until we can find her a new home."

"I miss you, Dad. Can I come and visit you?" she asked. "Meet your cats?"

"Sure. When can you come?"

"After my exams, I have a week in June before I have to start my summer job."

"Text me the dates, and I'll arrange a ticket. We can invite Zoey and her friend Axel to join us. I promised them a fishing trip."

"Yeah, it would be good to see Zoey too. Thanks, Dad."

He waited for her to hang up, but he heard her talking to Marlene, so he stayed on the line until Marlene came on.

"Lance, she got home last night, and I intended to call you this morning. Then I had a call from a client, and—"

He took a deep breath and told himself not to engage. "It's okay, Marlene. I'm just glad she got home safe."

"Thanks. I appreciate your understanding." Then she added, "And thanks for backing me up just now. Chelsea is already being kinder."

"You know I always have your back. That's never changed."

"I just forgot that for a while. I'm sorry. I should go and make sure she gets to her afternoon classes."

"Goodbye, Marlene." He hung up and stretched. The stress of not knowing Chelsea's whereabouts dissipated. His conversation with Marlene had gone better than any since they stopped seeing the mediator.

Maybe, when he looked back in a few years, he would even describe their divorce as amicable.

Mrrowww. Rhett Butler leaped up on the bed, pawing at him.

"Coming, boss." He rose, and Rhett scampered to the other end of the hall to wait for breakfast with Tilly and continue their relaxed new routine. Yes, he reflected as he poured the cat food into two bowls, his family looked a little different now, but they were still his family. He could let go of regrets and anger and finally move forward with his new life. It had room for everything he loved: his girls, fishing, books, cats… and a certain cat woman.

She just didn't know it yet.

CHAPTER 19

*R*aven chose a domestic shorthair with black, brown, and ginger stripes to adopt out next. Rosalyn had found him on the doorstep of her vet practice, along with a note from the owner that said they could no longer care for him.

There was no name on the note—or on the cat. So Rosalyn and her staff named him Phoenix. "We thought he could rise out of the ashes of his old life," said Rosalyn, when she had dropped off the cat two weeks earlier.

"Are you getting cornier as you age?" asked Raven. "Or is it just my imagination?"

Rosalyn laughed. "Make fun all you want. He seems to like his new name." And she was correct. The cat seemed to know when he was being called. Perhaps he, too, wanted a fresh start.

She understood the feeling. She wanted to stop digging in the past and start figuring out what—and who—she wanted in her life. Now that the cat project had started off so well, she had time to consider her future. And she decided that, after years of looking after cats and children, she wanted more.

As she dressed in her best jeans and a new T-shirt, she took the time to look in the mirror. It was good thing Rosalyn wasn't here. She would have teased Raven mercilessly about dressing up, yet again, to go to the bookstore.

"Shut it," she said to the imagined Rosalyn—who was laughing again. She packed the cat into the car and headed for her destination.

When she arrived, the store was closed, but Lance greeted her immediately, took the cat carrier, and placed it on the chair where she had put Sea Smoke only a few days before.

"Hello," he said, his bright smile indicating that he was genuinely pleased to see her. "Who have we here?"

She took the sheet from her tote bag. "This is Phoenix. I brought some information about him for the window."

He opened the display, and she leaned in to remove Tilly's information, but it wasn't there. "Where's the information about Tilly?" she asked, after slipping Phoenix's details into the window display. "I was wondering why people weren't calling about her. She's such a sweet cat—I thought she would be gone in only a few days."

"About that," said Lance, looking rather sheepish. But he didn't have a chance to say anything more because they were interrupted by his aunt's strong voice.

"Raven, I'm glad I caught you. I've come for an update."

Raven turned around. "Hi, Betty. I wasn't expecting you to be here." Raven was genuinely happy to see the older woman, in part because focusing on Betty meant she could avoid looking at Lance again. He looked entirely too good in his black T-shirt and jeans, and she found it difficult to look at anything else.

"I came to see how our little experiment was going, and to let Lance know I'm on my way to England for three weeks. I have a cousin there I haven't seen in years, and she invited me to her daughter's wedding."

"That sounds like fun," said Raven. "Are you going on your own?"

"Hah! My daughter would have none of that. She's coming with me, and I think she's looking forward to it. I imagine my schedule will be organized to the minute, but I am determined to have fun anyway." She laughed good-naturedly.

Raven shared in her laughter a moment, pleased that her friend was going to have quality time with her daughter. She loved it when Wren was in town. "As for your update, I am very pleased with things on my end. We've had one adoption and a lot of interest so far, though we apparently need to review our processes and make sure we work out any kinks. I could have sworn I put Tilly's information in the window."

"You did," said Lance. "I took it out again."

"Why?"

"I believe," said Betty, chuckling, "that my nephew is trying to tell you that Tilly has already found a home."

"You caught me," said Lance.

"Am I missing something?" asked Raven, looking from Betty's delighted face to Lance's red one.

"Raven, I've been keeping Tilly in the office with me most of the day. She doesn't seem to like being around all the people, and at night, well, she keeps Rhett company."

Betty shook her head at him. "You have always been a soft touch, my boy."

"In my defense, adopting her was Rhett's idea." He looked down to where the cat in question was rubbing against his legs. "He seems to like taking care of her, and the pair of them curl up on my sofa every night. He has become very protective."

Raven laughed out loud. "Aren't you the guy who hates cats?"

"Let's just say they're growing on me." He bent down to give Rhett Butler a scratch behind the ears.

"Tell me how everything else is going," said Betty. "I have to leave in a few minutes to get home before Nancy gets there. She is determined I need help packing, and is aghast that I haven't started even though we don't leave for another three days."

"We're getting a lot of hits on the website," said Raven. "Especially on the link to the webcam. The 'Tumble Twins' are popular. In a few weeks they will be old enough to adopt out, but I'd like to offer them as a sibling pair. They seem inseparable."

"We are getting daily inquiries about cats here in the store. Which reminds me: we'll need more brochures and info cards soon."

"I have some in the car," said Raven. "Left over from my latest parent-teacher education session. I'll get them for you before I leave."

"How many sessions have you done?" asked Betty, looking up at them and beaming. She must have been pleased about her trip, Raven reflected. But it was nice that she still had an interest in the project.

"Two, and I have another two scheduled before the end of the school term. People have been very receptive."

"It sounds like a promising start," said Betty, looking pointedly at Lance. "And how are book sales?"

"I get a few people coming in to see cats, and once they're here, they're browsing. According to the records, we seem to be up about twenty percent from last year. Ahmed and I have talked about other spinoff ideas we could put into place too. And our adoption day at the end of the month will hopefully help the bottom line."

"Good to see things are going as expected," said Betty. "I knew I was leaving the store in good hands. Now, Lance. Why don't you let Raven put the new cat in his pen out back, and you can help me get to my car."

"I'll be back in a few minutes, Raven," said Lance, picking up the deposit bag for the bank and handing her the swipe key to get into the back room. "Would you mind locking the door behind me?" Then he opened the door for his aunt and walked with her down the street.

Raven watched him go and realized though he would only be gone a few minutes,

she couldn't wait for him to come back,

"Well, Phoenix," she said, "Let's get you settled in."

CHAPTER 20

*L*ance walked beside Betty, who was easily running her motorized wheelchair without assistance. "Did you want to talk to me about something?" he asked. She clearly didn't need his help getting into her van. It was customized for her, and she had been driving it for years.

"I just wanted to ask you to be careful with Raven," said Betty. "She is more fragile than you know."

"What are you on about?" he asked. "Raven can hold her own from what I've seen."

Betty sighed. "I just want you to be careful not to hurt her. It's clear that she likes you."

"I like her too. She's nice."

"Lance, what I mean to say is she is interested in you. Her gaze follows you around the room."

"Really?" said Lance, grinning at Betty. "I hadn't noticed."

"You little…," said Betty. "The feeling is mutual, isn't it? You like her too!"

"More than I like cats, and I let them live with me," said Lance. "I find her easy to talk to, and interesting. But I will take care not to hurt her if that's what you're worried about."

"And take care of your own heart, Lance. It hasn't been that long."

"It's been a year and a half. Marlene is getting married again, and though it was a shock that she was marrying my friend, I wish them well. "

"You never told me that she was seeing your friend."

"I didn't know—until they announced their engagement."

"Are you all right?"

"Yes. As I say, I wish them well."

"And how are you finding it? Being back here, I mean. Any regrets?"

"I've not been here a month, but I feel like I belong for the first time in years. I'm glad I came to Sunshine Bay. It feels like the home I've been seeking for far too long. And did I tell you the girls are both going to visit me soon? Zoey already likes it here."

Betty reached up and squeezed his arm. "I am glad, my boy. It is good to have you back and to see you happier again." He stood beside her for a long minute until she said, "I must go. Nancy will be waiting."

She reached into a pocket in the chair and pulled out her car keys and the remote control for her ramp. He stepped back while she boarded the van and closed the door behind her. "Have a great trip," he said, waving as she drove away. She tooted goodbye on the horn.

He continued up the street to the bank to make his evening deposit. When he returned to the store, he found Raven in the back room getting water for Phoenix. "Did you find everything okay?" he asked.

"He's got everything he needs," she said. "I'll just go out and get the pamphlets."

"Have you had dinner?"

"No, not yet."

"I thought I would go down to the water and get fish and chips from that little place on the wharf. Would you like to join me?"

"Umm…" She looked up at him.

"Sorry, I didn't mean anything by it," he said, remembering Betty's warning. "I just thought since we haven't eaten and it's a nice evening, maybe we could go together and talk about the adoption day a bit. It's only two weeks from now."

She looked at him a few more moments then said, "Sure. I haven't had fish and chips since last summer. I'd like that."

CHAPTER 21

When Raven and Lance arrived at the little fish and chip café, they found a table overlooking the bay and Lance went to order their food.

"Thanks for the suggestion," she said when he returned with two cans of soda. "It's really nice here."

"One of the by-products of living in a beautiful place is that, after a while, we tend to take them for granted," he said.

"Yes, I suppose it's the same with everything that becomes too familiar," said Raven. "We don't always appreciate things or people until they leave."

"I know what you mean," said Lance. "I've missed my girls a lot in the past several months. That's why it was so good to have Zoey visit last week. And Chelsea will be coming to see me in a few weeks as well."

"And your wife? Do you miss her?" She had to ask. Though he had been separated for nearly two years, she knew from experience that it could be hard to let go.

"You know, I thought I would," he said. "But no. I miss having a partner, but I don't miss Marlene. We grew apart years ago. What about you? Did you miss your ex?"

"Duane?" She laughed. "No, I was glad to see the back of him. But being a single parent was hard. I did miss having help until Rosalyn and I joined forces."

"So you've let go of Duane? I remember you expressing some anger toward him the first time we spoke."

"You remember that?"

"I remember everything about you," he said. "I guess you make an impression." Their order number was called then, and he excused himself to go and pick it up. When he returned with their food, she thanked him, and they ate in silence for a few minutes.

"You're right. I do have anger toward Duane. But mostly it is anger at myself."

"Why were you angry at yourself?" he asked, dipping a thick potato chip in ketchup and eating it.

"Until I was thirteen, I lived on a small island with my family and two other families. We farmed and fished and lived off the land. My mother made sure we did our school lessons every day, and my parents had a huge library that we supplemented with library books from the nearest town, which was two hours away by boat."

"Sounds isolated."

"It was. But we learned how to be self-reliant. How to look after animals and gardens and each other. And once our mail-order business started—you remember those, before the internet." She smiled. "Well, I pitched in on that too. Everyone on the island was part of one community, and we needed each other to survive. And then I went to the nearest town for school."

"What was that like?"

"Well, it was lonely, and I missed my father. My sister and mother and I moved off the island, and my mother made sure we finished high school and encouraged us to get a trade. I think she thought we would return to the island and live there, bringing back skills to help run the business. But instead, I got married to Duane. Had a child and, as far as my mother was concerned, betrayed her. Or at least that was what I thought for years."

"How so?"

"Duane was extremely self-centered. Everything was about keeping up appearances and doing things he thought were right. Including rare visits to see my parents and using my management skills to start and run his business." She laughed. "When we divorced, I think he was genuinely surprised that I got half the assets. Though I had managed all the details, I don't think he truly appreciated the work I did."

"That's unfortunate," said Lance.

"He kept me away from my parents and kept our daughter away as well. I wish I had understood that earlier."

"What happened to your parents?"

"They retired to Mexico. They visit once a year, usually in August when it's still warm up here. After I left Duane, we were able to make amends, but it was hard. My parents warned me about him, but I knew best."

"You have your daughter," said Lance.

"That's true."

"And you never wanted to remarry?"

"My daughter and the business became my focus. And besides, I never really found anyone who interested me," she said.

Until now.

They walked back to her car in silence, pausing when they got to the boardwalk above the wharf to watch the sunset. When they arrived at the car, she opened the back to grab the pamphlets.

"Thanks," he said, taking them from her but not stepping away from the car. She closed the hatchback and leaned on it. She needed something to hold on to if he was going to stay where he was.

"Raven," he said, "I had a good time tonight, and I was wondering if you would ever consider going on a date with me."

"I think that's what we just did," said Raven, her voice breathy. Why was her voice breathy? She took a deep breath, trying to calm the wild banging in her chest.

"No, a date is different," said Lance.

"How so?" Her breathy voice was still there.

"Well, most dates I've been on involved a good-night kiss," he said.

"Oh," she said. Her eyes searched his. "And that's all that stands between what we did this evening and a date?"

"Yes." He was closer now. How did that happen?

"So, if you took me on a real date, you would want to kiss me?" She looked up at him, at his lips.

"Definitely," those lovely lips said.

"Well, I wouldn't want to waste your time," she whispered.

He cocked his head. "Explain your thinking,"

"If we kiss now, then we'll know whether or not we'd like to go on a second date."

"True." His weight shifted, and he was nearly touching her now. "I'm all for not wasting time," he said. "If you're game, that is."

"Seems the smart thing to do." She said, her tongue dampening her lips.

"Well, I'm also all for doing smart things." He leaned and put the package of brochures on the roof of the car. "Shall we?"

"Uh-huh." Raven leaned toward him. He braced his hands against the hatchback of her car, trapping her in his arms, and leaned in.

She closed her eyes as his lips swooped in and caught hers, gently and then more urgently. Her arms went up around his back seemingly of their own volition, and she pulled herself closer, the kiss now hungry.

She clung to him, not wanting to let go. But eventually he stepped back and released her. Her eyes fluttered open to find his hot gaze on her.

"So... another date, then?" he asked.

"Definitely," she said.

"Oh, good," he said. "Because I'd hate to fall for someone who kissed like that but didn't want me."

"Fall?" she asked.

"Well, it's early days, Raven," he said, rubbing his hand over his short hair. "And we haven't known each other long."

"No, though we know each other quite well considering it's only been a couple of weeks."

"And I've been attracted to you ever since you charged after Sebastien on the ferry that day."

"Really?"

"I don't bandage up everyone's cat scratches, you know. Just beautiful women I want to know better."

"Well, you can bandage up my scratches any day, Mr. Reed."

He chuckled. "In your line of work, that may be quite often."

"Let's hope so," she said, kissing him again.

CHAPTER 22

The last Saturday in June, Raven knocked on the window of the bookstore and waved at Lance.

He smiled, waved back, and walked over to unlock the door.

"Good morning," he said, leaning down to kiss her.

"Mmmm, good morning. Sorry I'm late."

"You're not late. Mrs. Albert won't be here for another hour," said Lance, referring to one of his regular customers. "I thought we could go for breakfast before we open."

"Are you sure this is a good idea? Do you think Mrs. Albert knows what she's getting herself into?"

"I spoke to her at length, explained the history, and even after all that, she seems determined. You and Mal are doing a great job of writing those profiles on your site."

"I just hope we don't get accused of false advertising," said Raven. "Though he does seem better."

"Well, let's take him to the back and see, shall we?" He took the cat carrier from Raven, and she followed. He put the carrier down on the floor and opened it, waiting for the cat to emerge. The cat stayed where he was, but there was no hissing today. "Is he still addicted to sardines?"

"He doesn't say no to them."

Lance opened a cupboard, pulled out some sardine-flavored cat treats, and put one outside the carrier. "Come on, boy."

Sebastien stuck his paw out toward the treat and tried to swipe it toward him, but it was just out of reach.

"Nope, you're going to have to come and get it," said Lance. The cat stepped out, quickly ate the treat, then walked toward Lance, who was holding out more tasty morsels. Sebastien took them, one at a time.

"He is much calmer than he was a month ago," said Lance. "You can tell by the pictures on your website. I think Mrs. Albert will like him. She's been following his story and seems to have fallen in love with our grumpy friend."

"She's single and doesn't have children," said Raven. "And as long as she isn't a closet party animal, it will be a nice, quiet place for him."

Lance reached out, and Sebastien allowed him to stroke his fur. Then he led the cat to a larger pen with a scratching post and a bed. "I must admit I have a soft spot for him. After all, I got new curtains because of him."

"Jerk," Raven laughed. "Though I probably never would have tried sewing if it hadn't been for that, and now I'm working on my first quilt."

"Sebastien says you're welcome."

"What time do you expect Chelsea?"

"Not until five o'clock tonight, and I pick up Zoey and

Axel at three tomorrow. We can get started right after closing."

"I'm looking forward to the trip," said Raven. "I haven't been fishing since I lived with my parents. Seems like a lifetime ago."

"Do you want to grab a coffee before I open?"

Raven looked at Sebastien. He had curled up in a corner and seemed happy enough. "Sure. If you let me buy this time."

They walked to Whisking Love, and Lance found a table while Raven went up to order the coffee. As she approached, she found Curtis chatting with Esther at the counter.

"Hello," Raven said. "How are you today?"

Curtis swiveled around to face her. "Great," he said, looking like a guilty schoolboy. "What brings you to town?"

"Came to deliver another cat," said Raven. "Just two coffees, please, Esther."

Esther went to get the cups, and Raven pulled her card out of her wallet. "How about you?"

"Me? I'm just here having breakfast with the boys."
Raven looked around the room. "They already left. I'm
just getting a takeaway lunch," he said. "How's the cat
display working out?" He nodded toward Lance.

"We've already found a spot for two and possibly three.
Pretty good for a week's work, I'd say." She tapped her
card at the pay terminal for the coffees Esther had just
placed in front of her. "Thanks again for your help."

"Not a problem," said Curtis. "See you soon."

Raven added cream to the coffees and joined Lance at
the table by the window. "Something's going on with
Curtis," she said.

"What do you mean?"

"When I went up to the counter to order, he acted as
though I'd caught him doing something wrong."

"Maybe he doesn't want anyone to know," said Lance,
taking a sip of the coffee.

"Know what?"

"That he likes Esther a bit more than he lets on."

"What?" Raven turned around. Curtis was leaning on

the counter, talking to Esther. They were laughing. "Hmm. Maybe you're right."

"Not sure about her, though," he said. "And it's none of my concern, so I would advise staying out of it."

"Well, I hope so," said Raven. "He deserves happiness after losing his wife so young."

"How is the application to establish your nonprofit going?"

"Okay, I get the picture. It's none of my business either," she said, turning to get one last glance at the couple at the counter. "But you may be right. He does seem happy right now."

Lance didn't say anything, just waited.

"The paperwork is done, and we have our new name. I even asked Zoey to do me up a logo. I'll put new signage on the window."

"What's the new name?"

"The Cat's Meow Rescue Centre."

Lance smiled. "I like it."

"Thanks," she said, pleased. "Once I get the new logo, I'll change signs, have her design me some templates for the forms and such. Axel is going to help me set up a way to accept donations on the site."

"He seems to have thrown himself into this wholeheartedly," said Lance. "I like him."

"Yes, and according to the last email I received from Zoey, he's pretty excited to be going fishing."

"I'm just glad that we both got the same time off. I'm glad you're joining us, and it will be nice for you to meet Chelsea."

"If she's anything like her sister, I'm confident we will get along well. Now tell me more about this boat. How big is it?"

Lance described Del's boat and the campsite they had arranged, and though she had been nervous to meet Chelsea and Del she was looking forward to it.

Lance's watch beeped. "I suppose it's time."

They rose and returned to the Bookworm.

ance introduced Raven to Mrs. Albert, who had arrived right on time, carrying an empty cat carrier and vibrating with anticipation.

"Is it appropriate?" she asked. "The man at the pet store said it would be large enough."

"It will work perfectly," Raven assured her as they led the woman to the back. When Mrs. Albert saw Sebastien, she set down the carrier and approached the pen slowly, bending down to peer at him through the wire mesh of the door.

"Aren't you lovely," she said.

Sebastien opened his eyes and looked at her, and Lance handed Mrs. Albert the package of treats he had on hand. "These are his favorites," he said. "Sebastien loves sardines."

Mrs. Albert turned to take the treats. "I like sardines too," she said. "Reminds me of my nana. She used to make sardines on toast for me when I was a child. I take this as a sign." She turned toward Sebastien, who was now standing and sniffing the air. "Yes, sir, I believe you and I will get along just fine."

Lance smiled up at Raven, and she grinned back. Then she helped Mrs. Albert put Sebastien into the carrier.

"I'll carry it to your car," Lance said.

"Thank you, son," said Mrs. Albert, handing back the package of treats.

"No, you keep them. I brought them in for Sebastien."

"And here is some information about Sebastien, and a coupon for ten percent off his next appointment at the vet up the street," said Raven. "And some food for him for the next two days."

Mrs. Albert put everything into her handbag. "Shall we?" she asked.

Lance saw the cat into the car, said farewell, then walked back to the store.

"You're right. She's a perfect match," said Raven. Lance bent down and gave her a quick kiss.

"Yes, perfect."

But he wasn't talking about the cat.

*a*uthor's Note:

Dear Reader,

I hope you enjoyed *The Bookworm and The Cat's Meow*. To read more of my books featuring cats, check out my Sunshine Bay series.

To read more about the downtown business owners at Sunshine Bay, try the rest of the Shops at Sunshine Bay series.

To stay up to date about my writing news, head over to my website at www.jeaninelauren.com to join my newsletter.

And until next time,

Happy Reading!

Jeanine

P.S.

If you liked Raven and Lance's story, please consider taking a few moments to leave a review. Reviews are a fabulous way to support an independent author like me so we can continue to write more books for you to enjoy.

Thank you!

ABOUT THE AUTHOR

Jeanine Lauren is a USA Today Bestselling author and has always loved a good story. She prefers those where the strength of community and the power of love combine to overcome even the darkest of situations.

And if there's a cat or dog in the story, all the better!

Jeanine writes from her home in the lower mainland of British Columbia, Canada, not far from the fictional town of Sunshine Bay, where many of her characters live.

Made in United States
Cleveland, OH
14 December 2024

11933973R00148